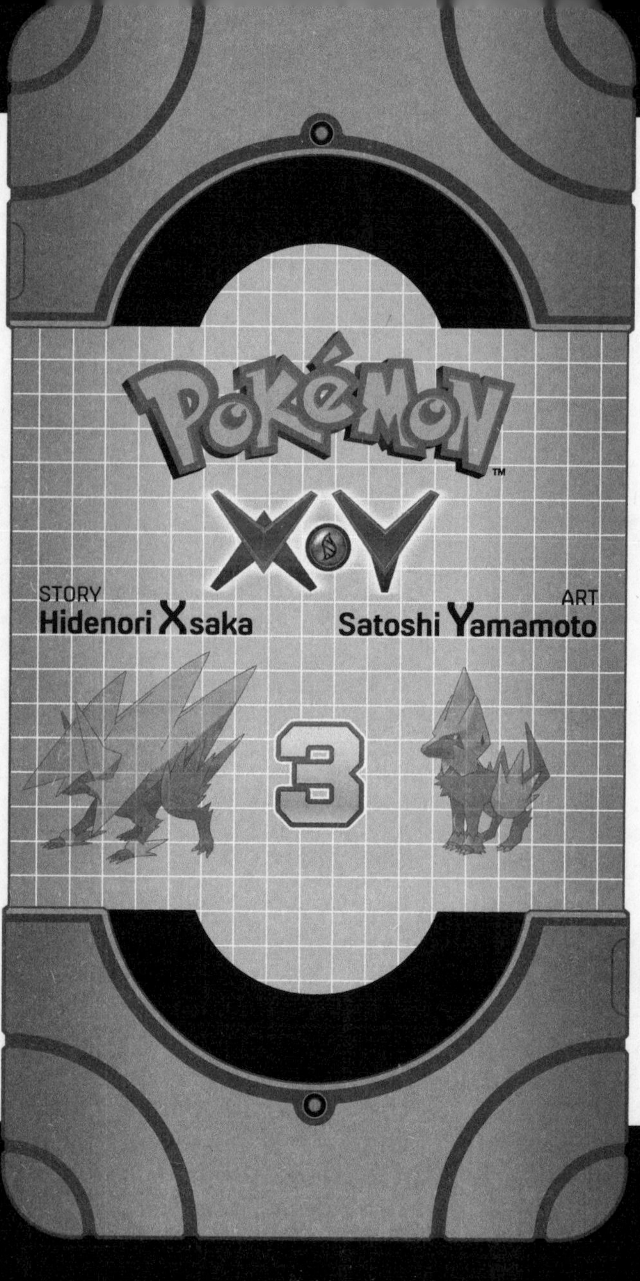

Pokémon™
X·Y
STORY
Hidenori Xsaka
ART
Satoshi Yamamoto
3

# CHARACTERS

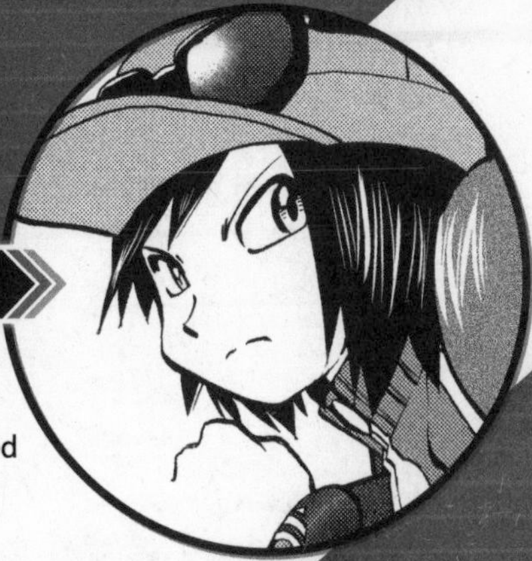

## X

The main character of this chapter, and one of five close childhood friends. He was once a highly skilled Trainer who even won the Junior Pokémon Battle Tournament, but now...

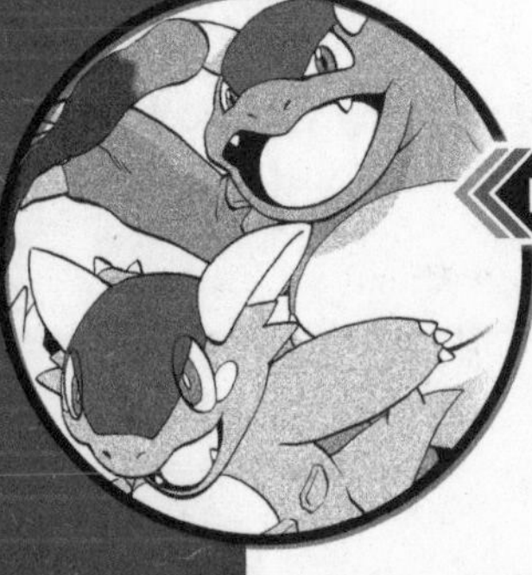

## KANGA & LI'L KANGA

X's longtime Pokémon partners with whom he won the Junior Tournament.

## OUR STORY THUS FAR...

In Vaniville Town in the Kalos region, X was a Pokémon Trainer child prodigy. But now he's depressed and hides in his room avoiding everyone—including his best friend Y. An attack on their hometown by Legendary Pokémon Xerneas and Yveltal, led by Team Flare, forces X outside... Now he and his closest childhood friends—Y, Trevor, Tierno and Shauna—are on the run!

Trouble arises in Santalune City when Shauna is mind-controlled by Team Flare scientist Celosia! Fortunately, X and a new ally, Shalour City Gym Leader Korinna, defeat Celosia and free Shauna. Now our friends must move on to the next town, with Team Flare in hot pursuit... Where will they end up next and what will befall them there...?

# MEET THE

## Y

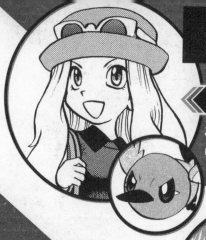

X's best friend, a Sky Trainer trainee. Her full name is Yvonne Gabena.

## TREVOR

One of the five friends. A quiet boy who hopes to become a fine Pokémon Researcher one day.

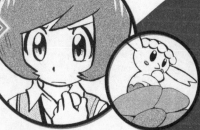

## SHAUNA

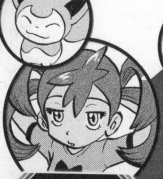

One of the five friends. Her dream is to become a Furfrou Groomer. She is quick to speak her mind.

## TIERNO

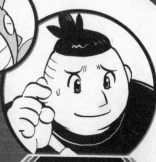

One of the five friends. A big boy with an even bigger heart. He is currently training to become a dancer.

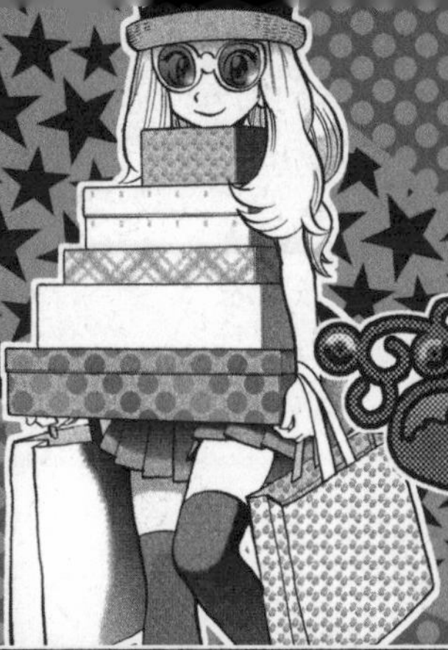

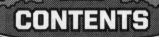

# CONTENTS



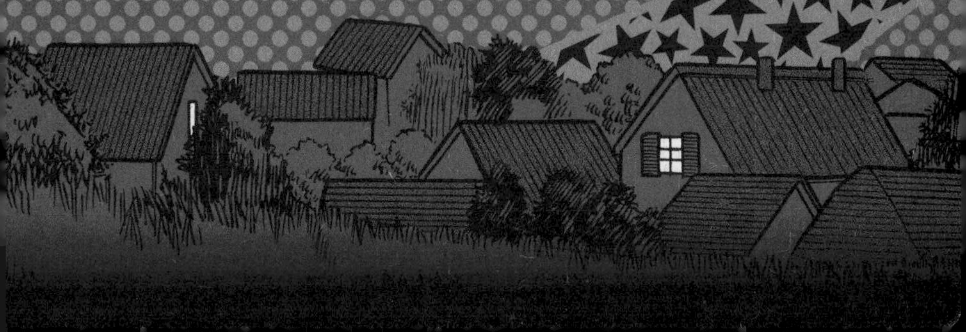

# Adventure 8 What Does Charmander Do When It Dozes?

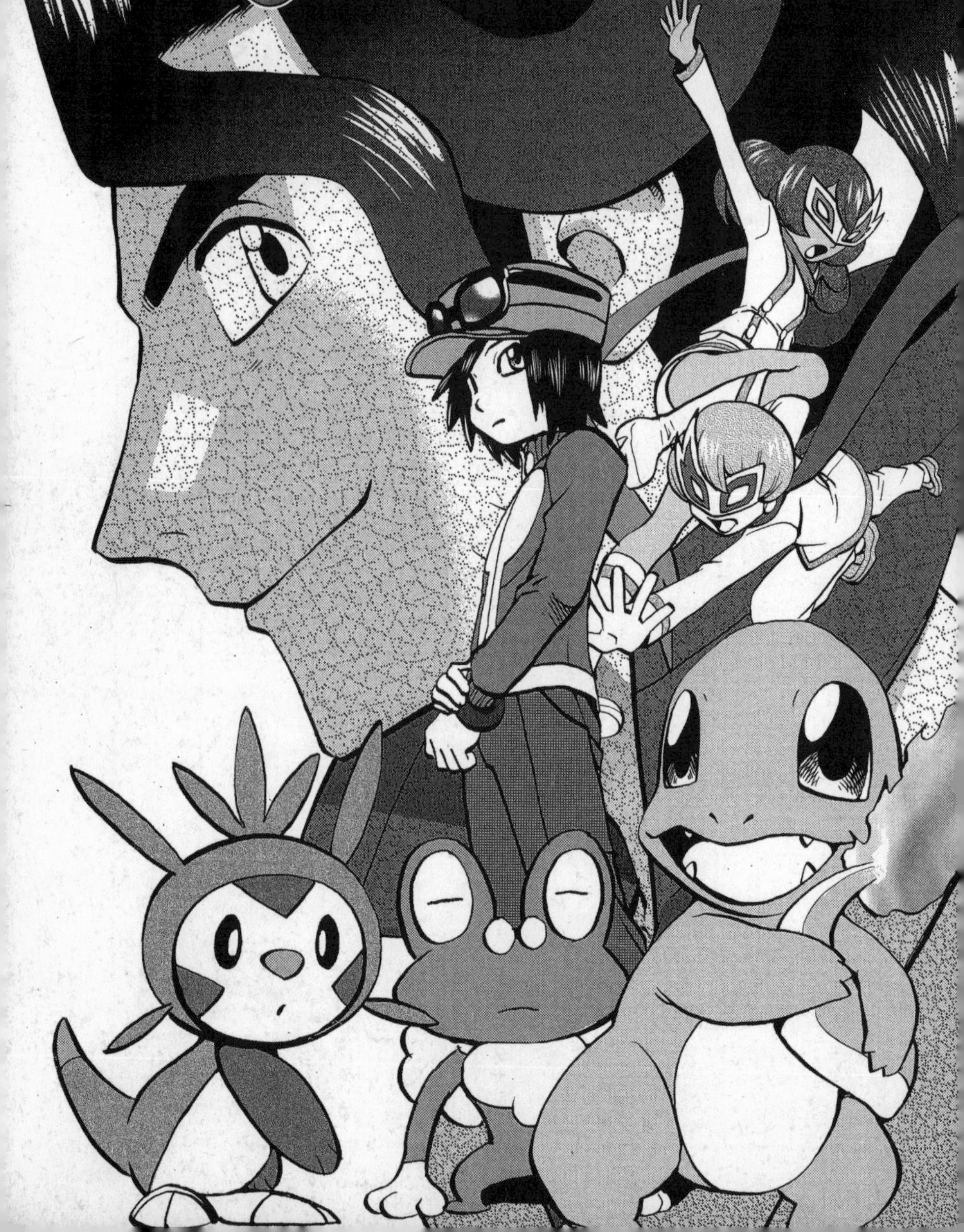

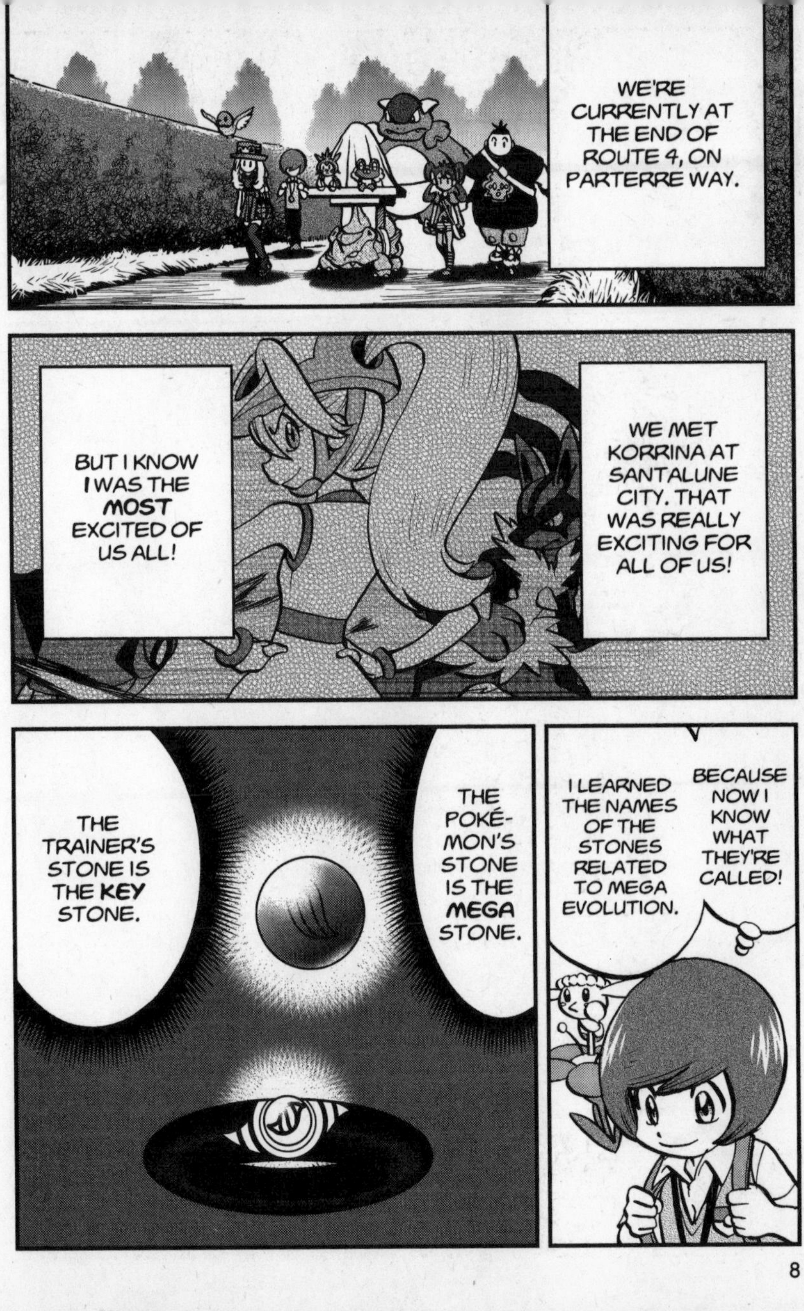
WE'RE CURRENTLY AT THE END OF ROUTE 4, ON PARTERRE WAY.
WE MET KORRINA AT SANTALUNE CITY. THAT WAS REALLY EXCITING FOR ALL OF US!
BUT I KNOW I WAS THE **MOST** EXCITED OF US ALL!
BECAUSE NOW I KNOW WHAT THEY'RE CALLED!
I LEARNED THE NAMES OF THE STONES RELATED TO MEGA EVOLUTION.
THE POKÉMON'S STONE IS THE **MEGA** STONE.
THE TRAINER'S STONE IS THE **KEY** STONE.

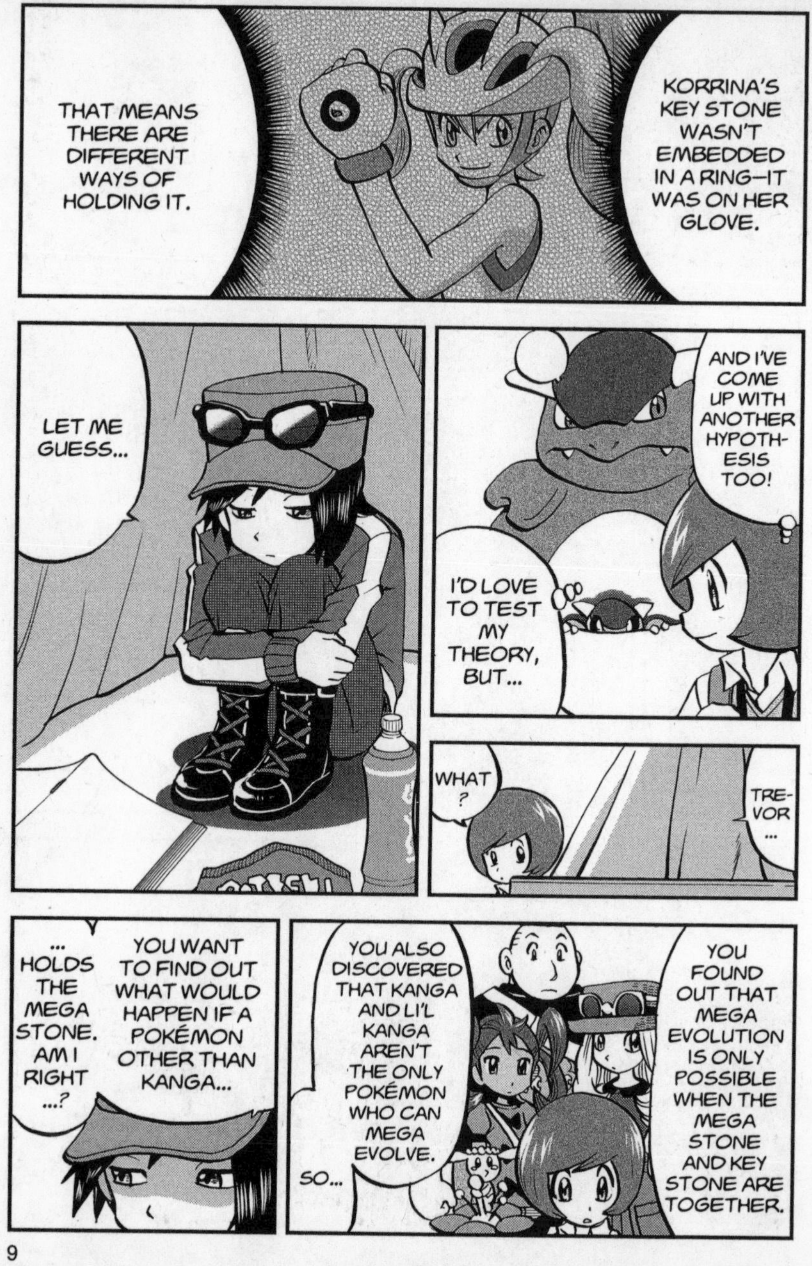
KORRINA'S KEY STONE WASN'T EMBEDDED IN A RING—IT WAS ON HER GLOVE.
THAT MEANS THERE ARE DIFFERENT WAYS OF HOLDING IT.
AND I'VE COME UP WITH ANOTHER HYPOTH-ESIS TOO!
I'D LOVE TO TEST MY THEORY, BUT...
TRE-VOR ...
WHAT ?
LET ME GUESS...
YOU FOUND OUT THAT MEGA EVOLUTION IS ONLY POSSIBLE WHEN THE MEGA STONE AND KEY STONE ARE TOGETHER.
YOU ALSO DISCOVERED THAT KANGA AND LI'L KANGA AREN'T THE ONLY POKÉMON WHO CAN MEGA EVOLVE.
SO...
YOU WANT TO FIND OUT WHAT WOULD HAPPEN IF A POKÉMON OTHER THAN KANGA...
... HOLDS THE MEGA STONE. AM I RIGHT ...?

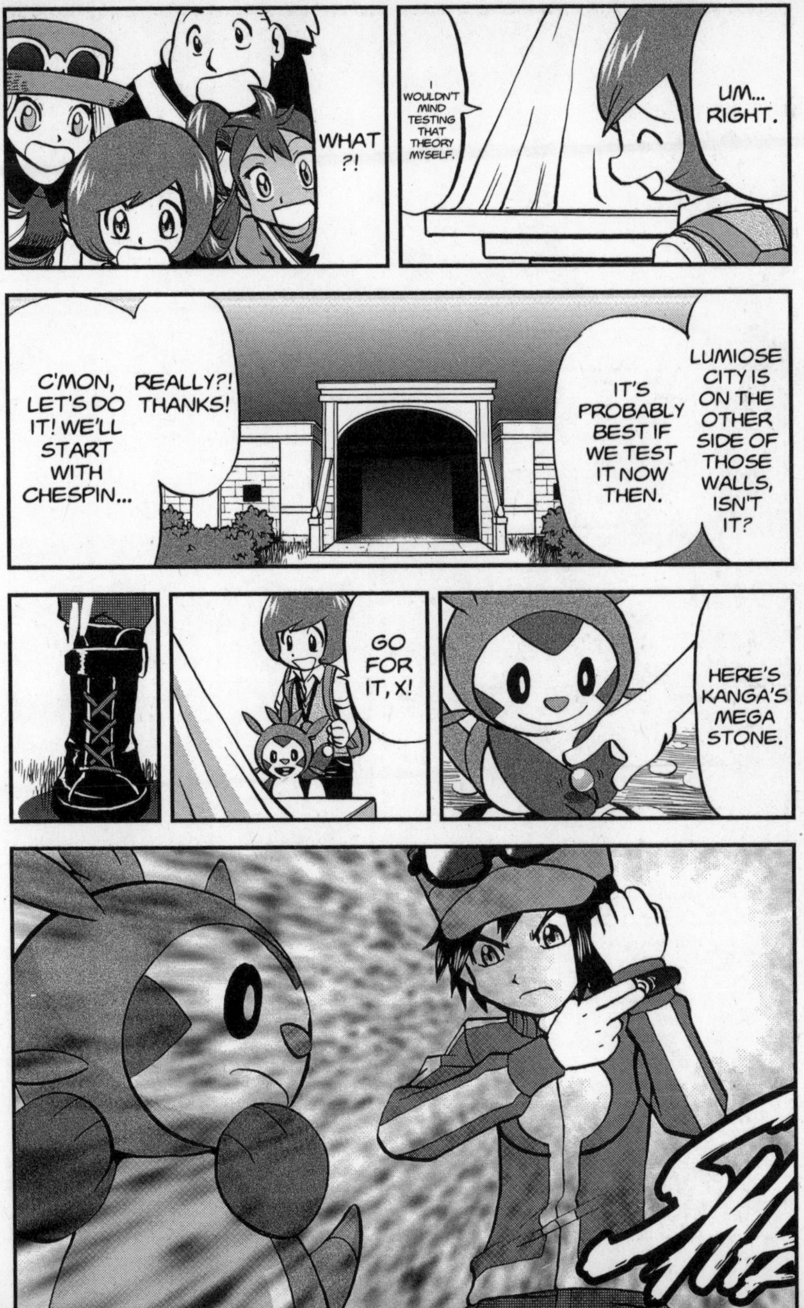
UM... RIGHT.
I WOULDN'T MIND TESTING THAT THEORY MYSELF.
WHAT?!
LUMIOSE CITY IS ON THE OTHER SIDE OF THOSE WALLS, ISN'T IT?
IT'S PROBABLY BEST IF WE TEST IT NOW THEN.
REALLY?! THANKS!
C'MON, LET'S DO IT! WE'LL START WITH CHESPIN...
HERE'S KANGA'S MEGA STONE.
GO FOR IT, X!

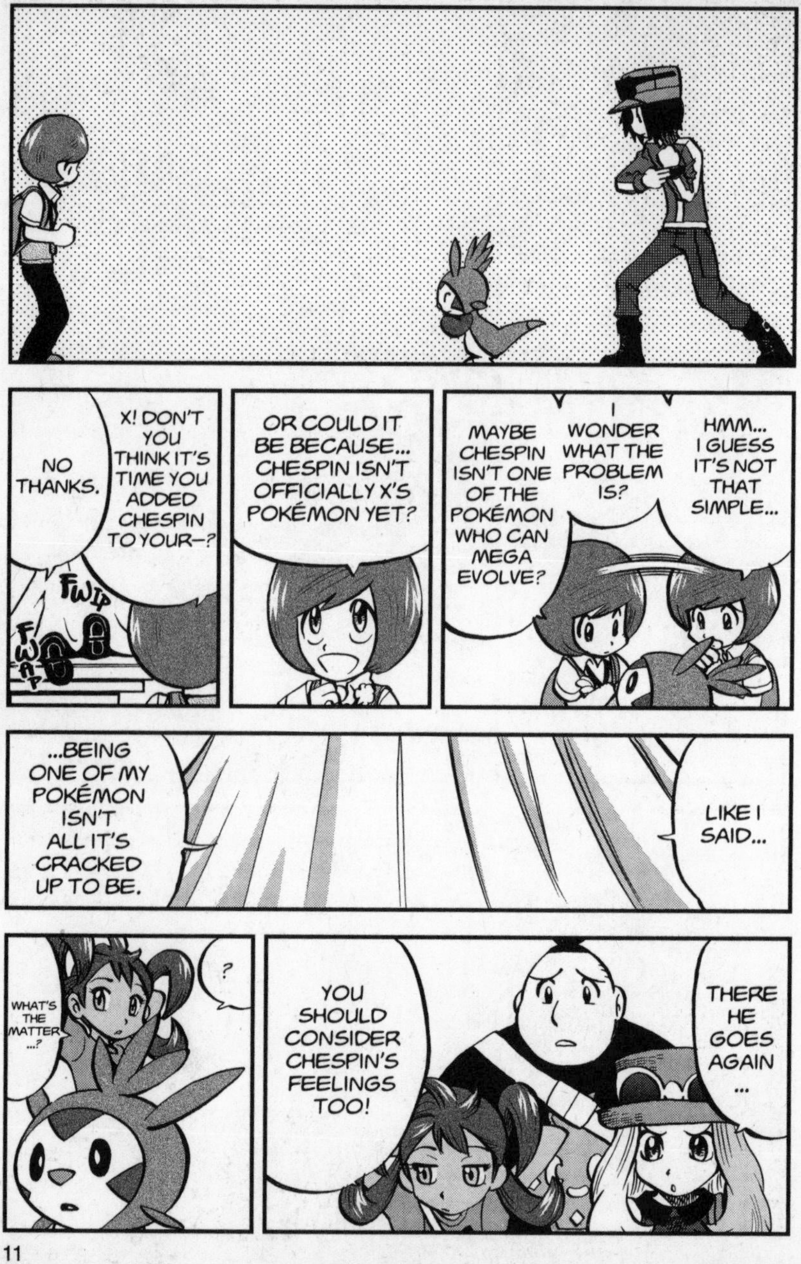
HMM... I GUESS IT'S NOT THAT SIMPLE...
I WONDER WHAT THE PROBLEM IS?
MAYBE CHESPIN ISN'T ONE OF THE POKéMON WHO CAN MEGA EVOLVE?
OR COULD IT BE BECAUSE... CHESPIN ISN'T OFFICIALLY X'S POKéMON YET?
X! DON'T YOU THINK IT'S TIME YOU ADDED CHESPIN TO YOUR—?
NO THANKS.
FWIP
FWAP
LIKE I SAID...
...BEING ONE OF MY POKéMON ISN'T ALL IT'S CRACKED UP TO BE.
THERE HE GOES AGAIN...
YOU SHOULD CONSIDER CHESPIN'S FEELINGS TOO!
?
WHAT'S THE MATTER...?

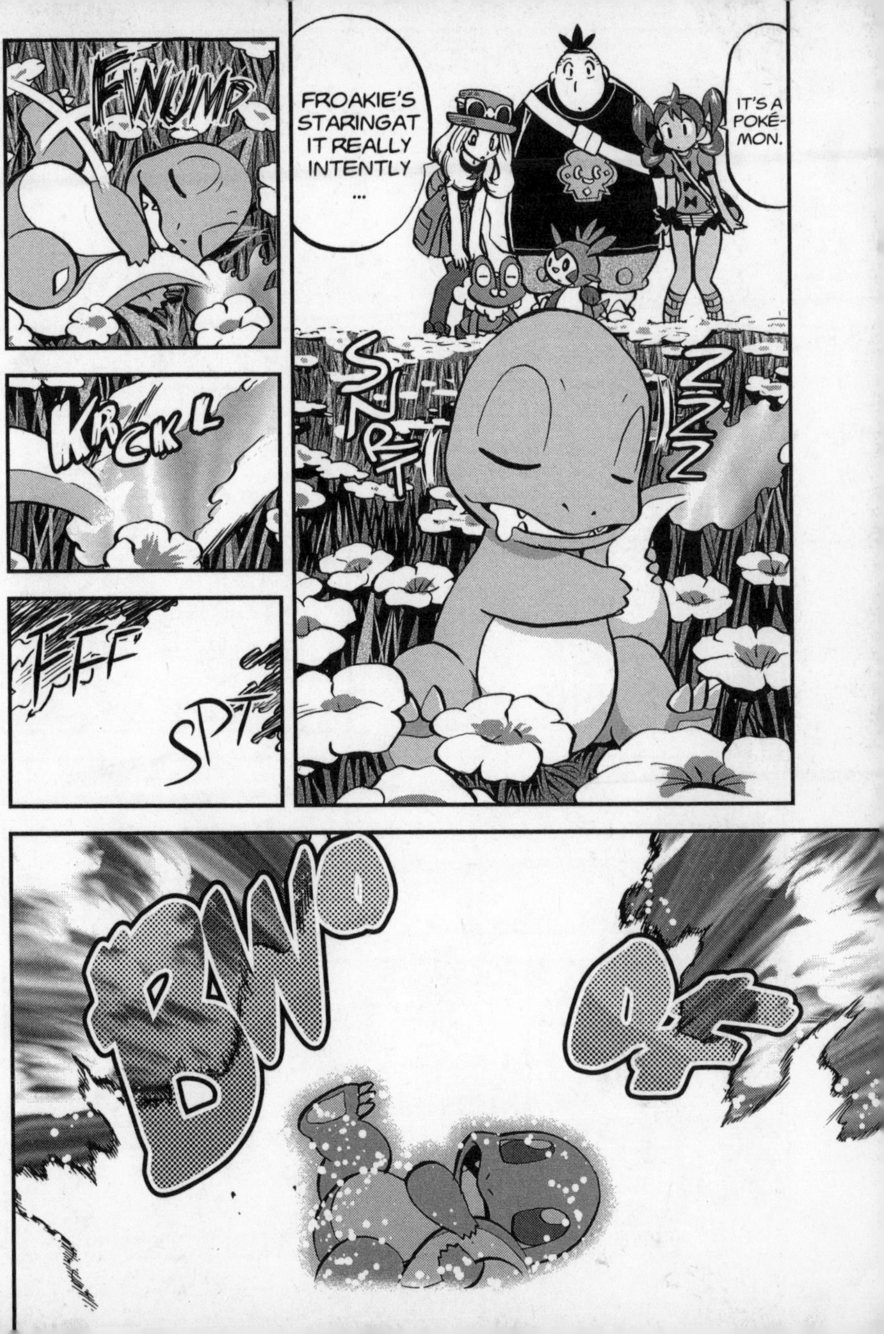
IT'S A POKÉ-MON.
FROAKIE'S STARINGAT IT REALLY INTENTLY ...
SNRT
ZZZ
FWUMP
KRCKL
FFF
SPT
BWOOF

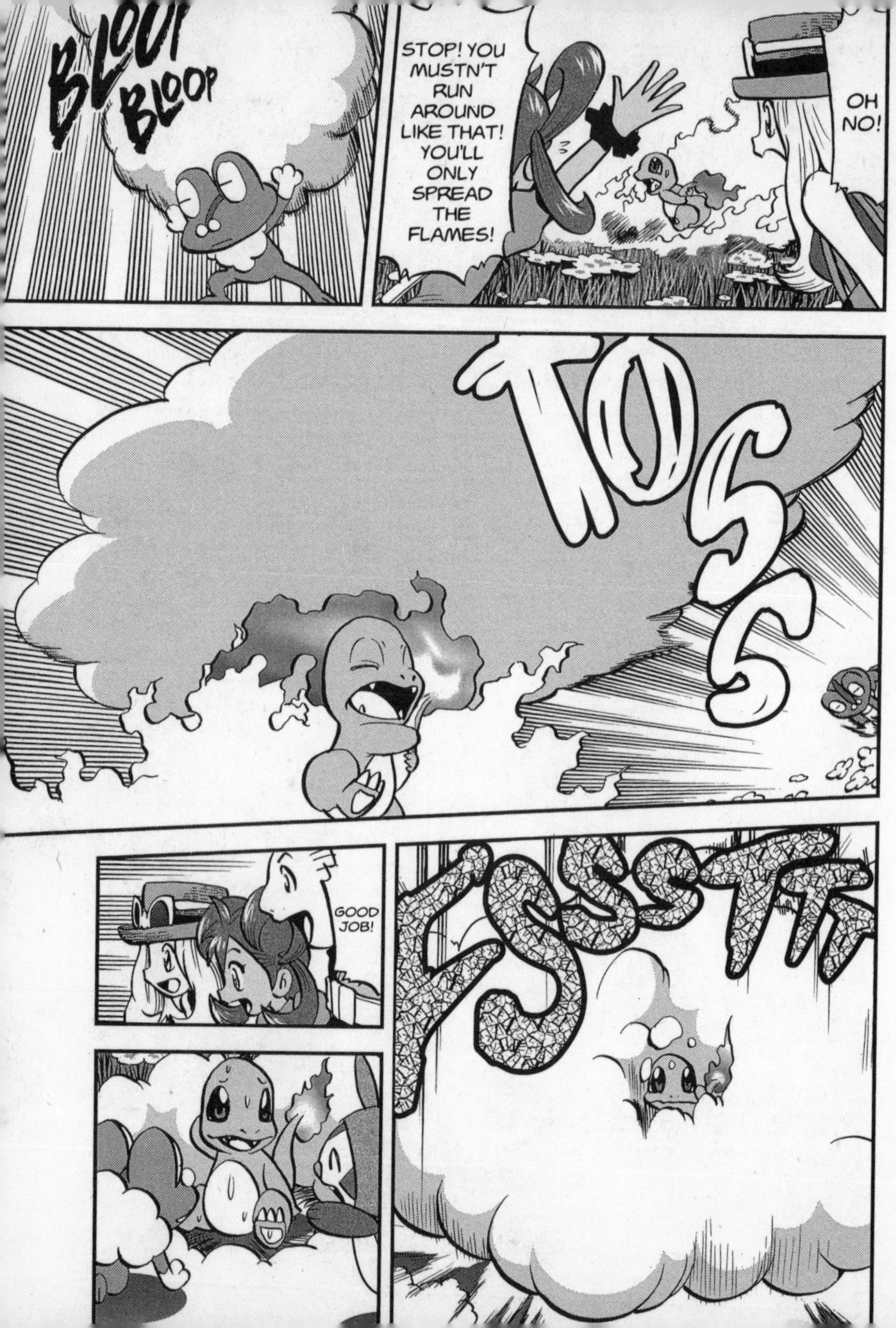
OH NO!
STOP! YOU MUSTN'T RUN AROUND LIKE THAT! YOU'LL ONLY SPREAD THE FLAMES!
BLOOP BLOOP
TOSS
FSSSTTT
GOOD JOB!

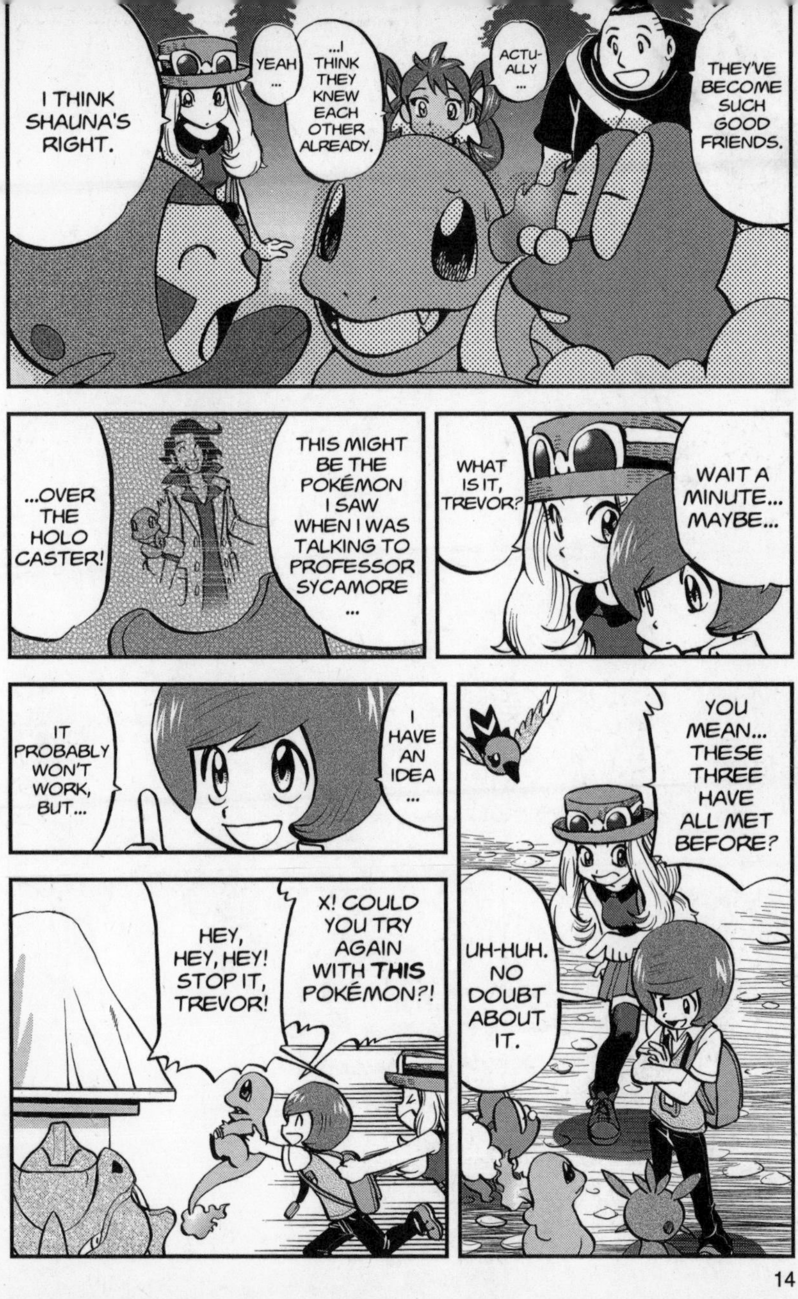
THEY'VE BECOME SUCH GOOD FRIENDS.
ACTU-ALLY...
...I THINK THEY KNEW EACH OTHER ALREADY.
YEAH...
I THINK SHAUNA'S RIGHT.
WAIT A MINUTE... MAYBE...
WHAT IS IT, TREVOR?
THIS MIGHT BE THE POKÉMON I SAW WHEN I WAS TALKING TO PROFESSOR SYCAMORE...
...OVER THE HOLO CASTER!
YOU MEAN... THESE THREE HAVE ALL MET BEFORE?
UH-HUH. NO DOUBT ABOUT IT.
I HAVE AN IDEA...
IT PROBABLY WON'T WORK, BUT...
X! COULD YOU TRY AGAIN WITH **THIS** POKÉMON?!
HEY, HEY, HEY! STOP IT, TREVOR!

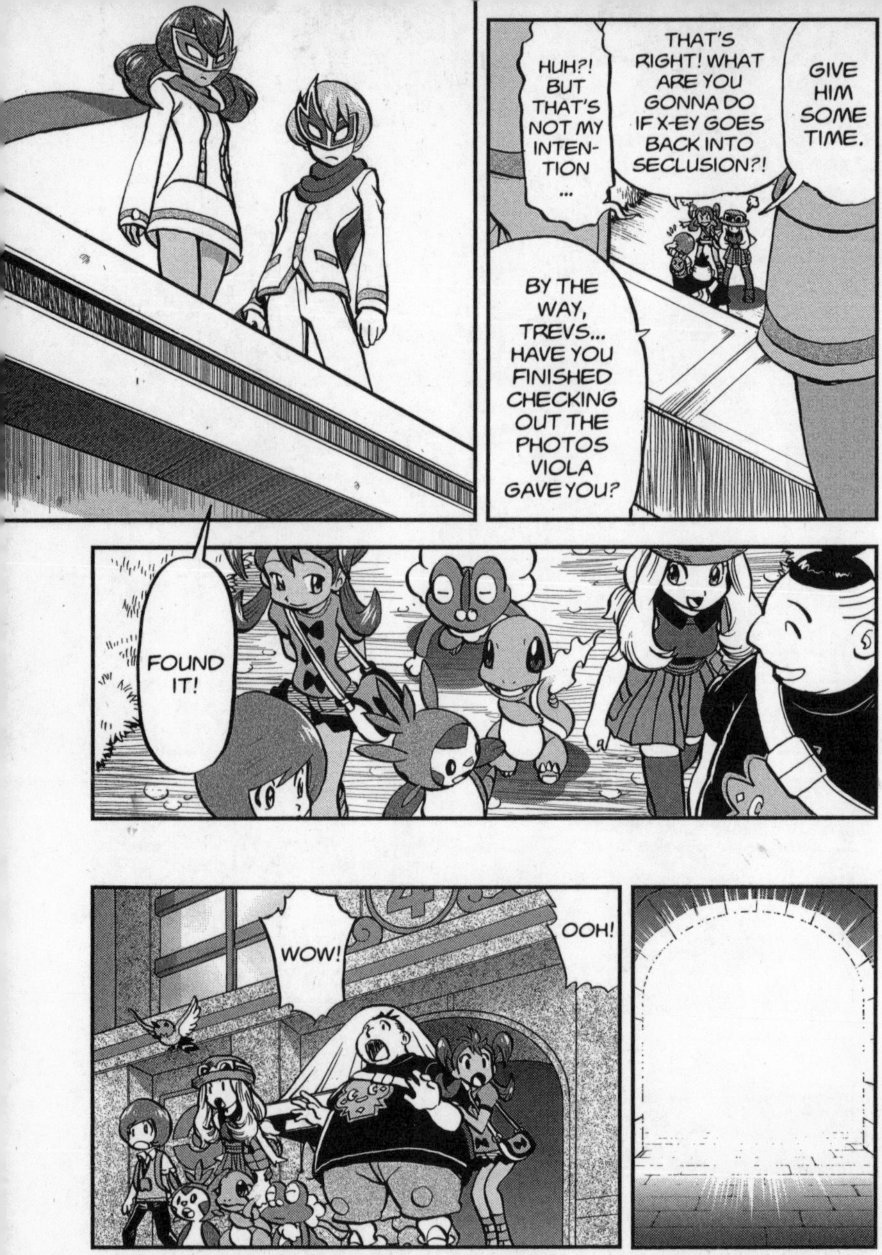
GIVE HIM SOME TIME.
THAT'S RIGHT! WHAT ARE YOU GONNA DO IF X-EY GOES BACK INTO SECLUSION?!
HUH?! BUT THAT'S NOT MY INTEN-TION ...
BY THE WAY, TREVS... HAVE YOU FINISHED CHECKING OUT THE PHOTOS VIOLA GAVE YOU?
FOUND IT!
OOH!
WOW!

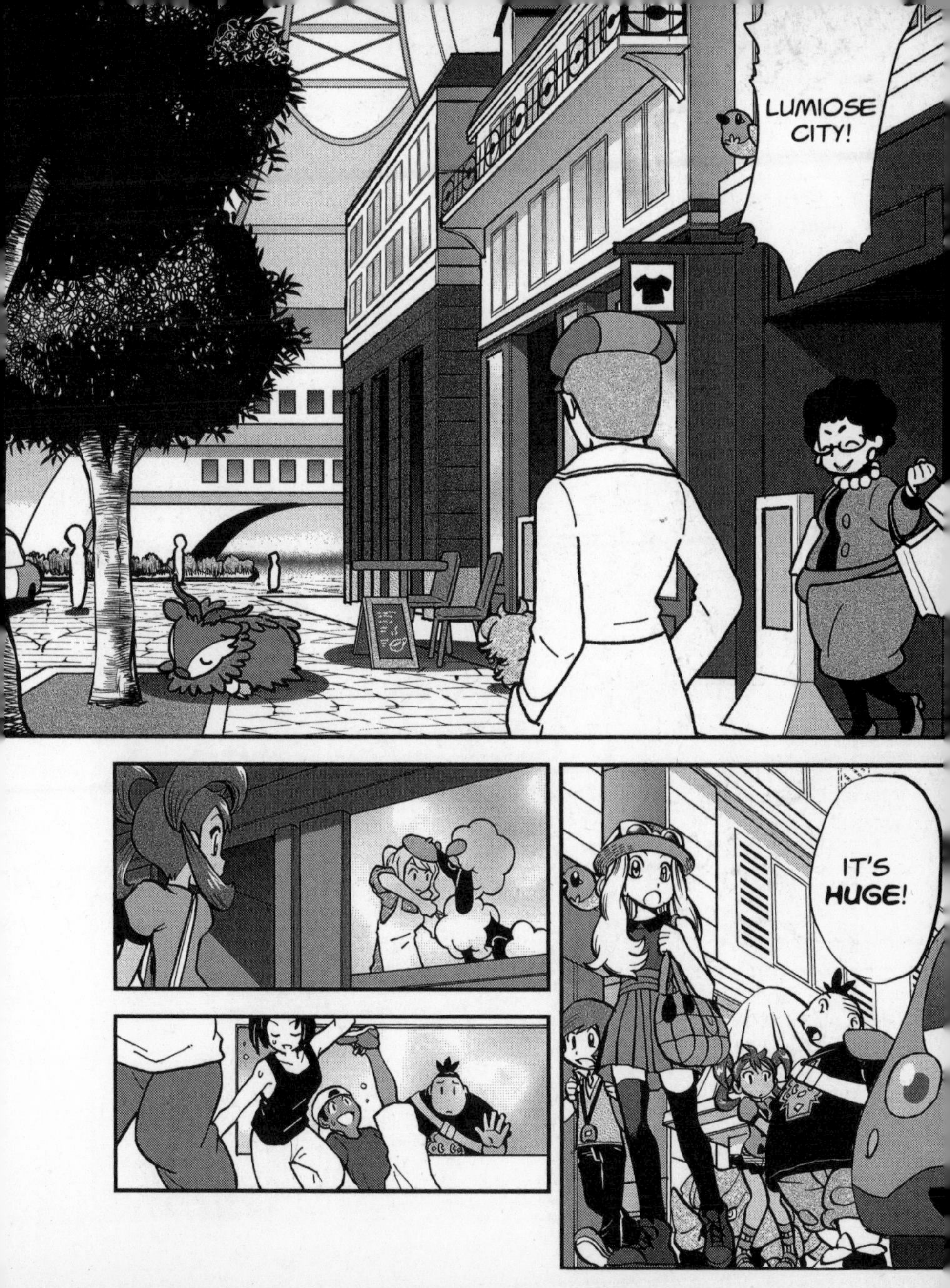
LUMIOSE CITY!
IT'S HUGE!

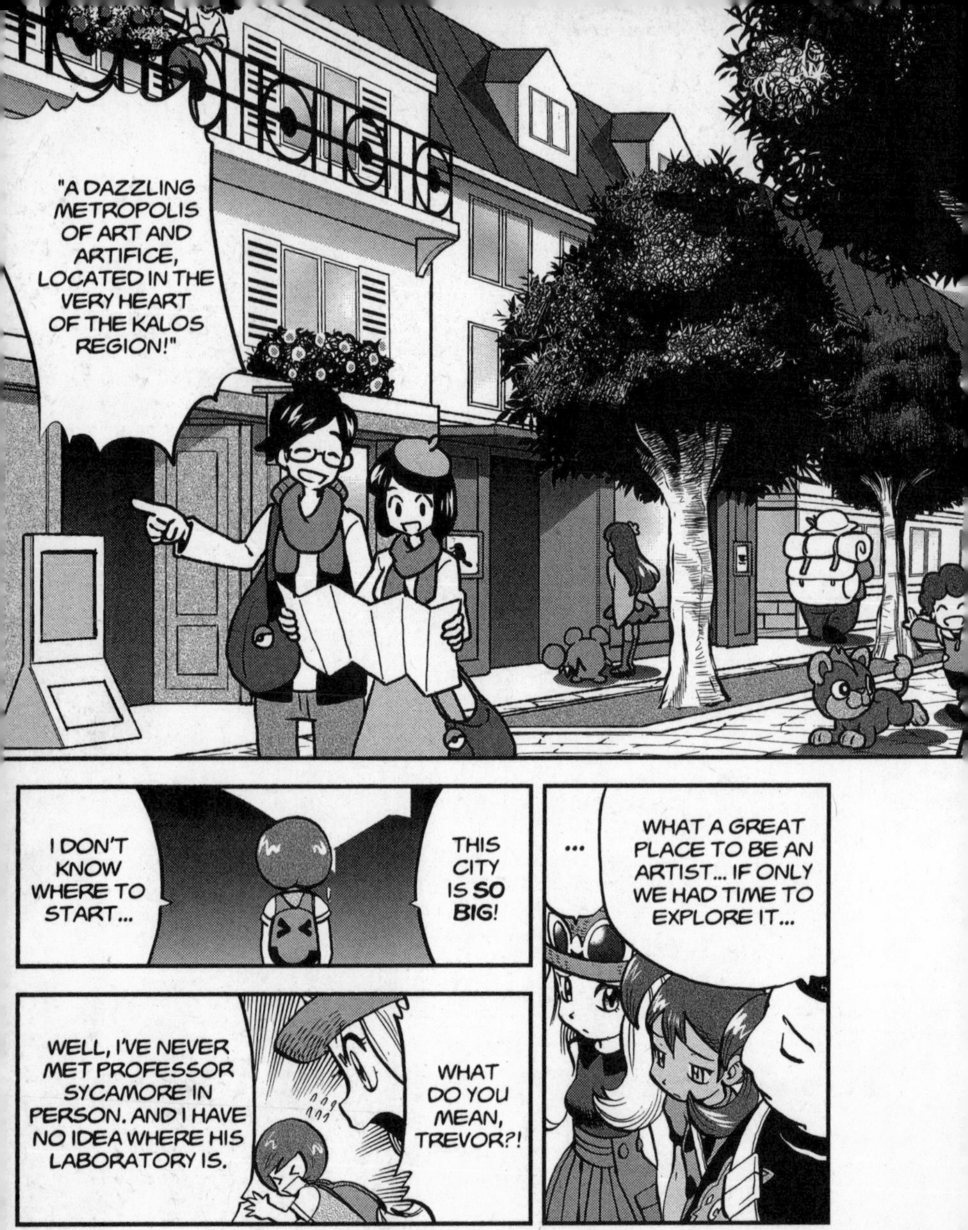
"A DAZZLING METROPOLIS OF ART AND ARTIFICE, LOCATED IN THE VERY HEART OF THE KALOS REGION!"
WHAT A GREAT PLACE TO BE AN ARTIST... IF ONLY WE HAD TIME TO EXPLORE IT...
...
THIS CITY IS **SO BIG**!
I DON'T KNOW WHERE TO START...
WHAT DO YOU MEAN, TREVOR?!
WELL, I'VE NEVER MET PROFESSOR SYCAMORE IN PERSON. AND I HAVE NO IDEA WHERE HIS LABORATORY IS.

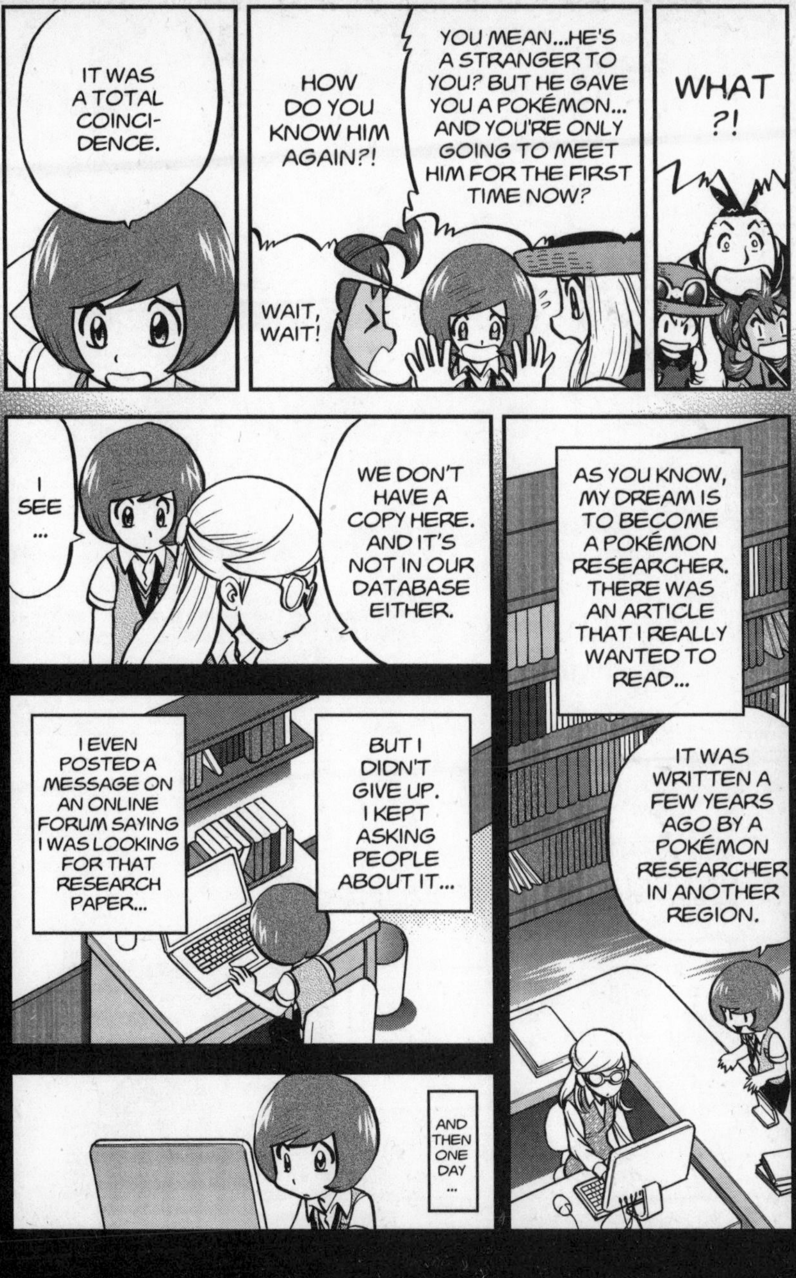
WHAT ?!
YOU MEAN...HE'S A STRANGER TO YOU? BUT HE GAVE YOU A POKÉMON... AND YOU'RE ONLY GOING TO MEET HIM FOR THE FIRST TIME NOW?
HOW DO YOU KNOW HIM AGAIN?!
WAIT, WAIT!
IT WAS A TOTAL COINCI-DENCE.
AS YOU KNOW, MY DREAM IS TO BECOME A POKÉMON RESEARCHER. THERE WAS AN ARTICLE THAT I REALLY WANTED TO READ...
IT WAS WRITTEN A FEW YEARS AGO BY A POKÉMON RESEARCHER IN ANOTHER REGION.
WE DON'T HAVE A COPY HERE. AND IT'S NOT IN OUR DATABASE EITHER.
I SEE ...
BUT I DIDN'T GIVE UP. I KEPT ASKING PEOPLE ABOUT IT...
I EVEN POSTED A MESSAGE ON AN ONLINE FORUM SAYING I WAS LOOKING FOR THAT RESEARCH PAPER...
AND THEN ONE DAY ...

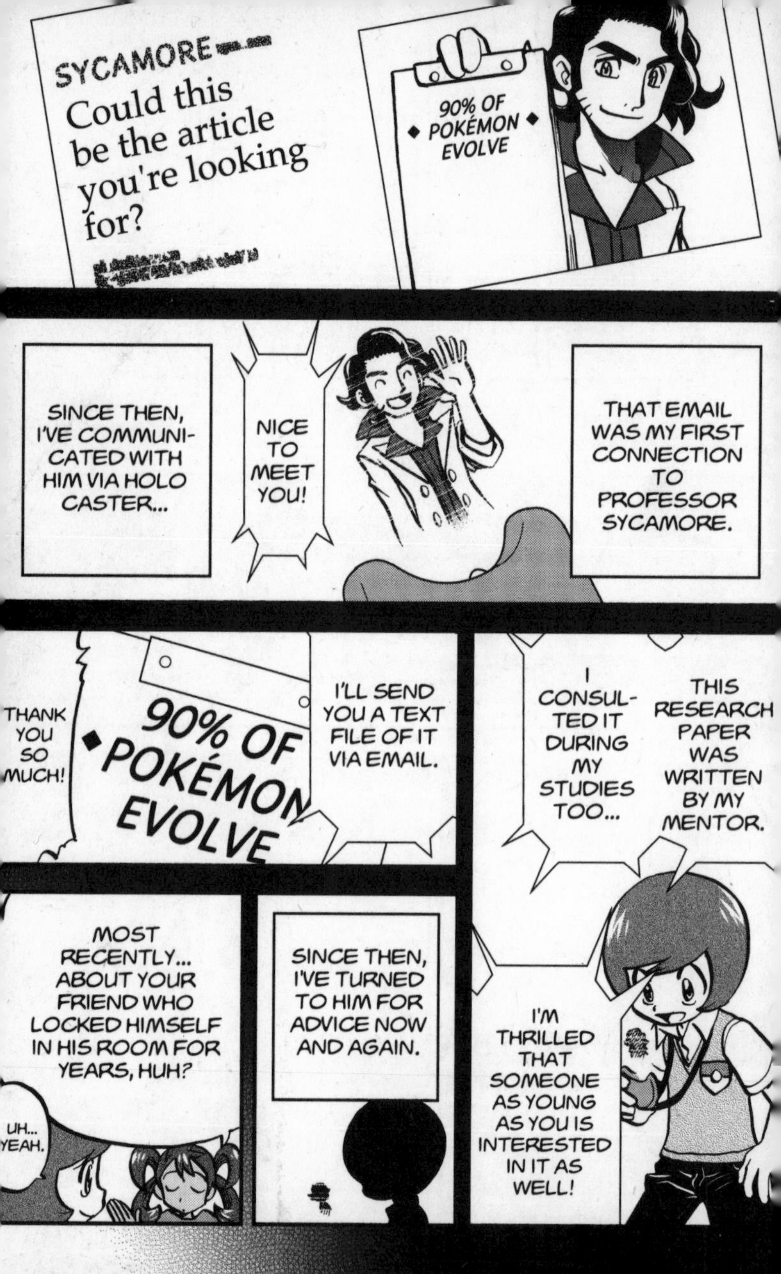
90% OF POKÉMON EVOLVE
SYCAMORE
Could this be the article you're looking for?
THAT EMAIL WAS MY FIRST CONNECTION TO PROFESSOR SYCAMORE.
NICE TO MEET YOU!
SINCE THEN, I'VE COMMUNICATED WITH HIM VIA HOLO CASTER...
THIS RESEARCH PAPER WAS WRITTEN BY MY MENTOR.
I CONSULTED IT DURING MY STUDIES TOO...
I'M THRILLED THAT SOMEONE AS YOUNG AS YOU IS INTERESTED IN IT AS WELL!
I'LL SEND YOU A TEXT FILE OF IT VIA EMAIL.
90% OF POKÉMON EVOLVE
THANK YOU SO MUCH!
SINCE THEN, I'VE TURNED TO HIM FOR ADVICE NOW AND AGAIN.
MOST RECENTLY... ABOUT YOUR FRIEND WHO LOCKED HIMSELF IN HIS ROOM FOR YEARS, HUH?
UH... YEAH.

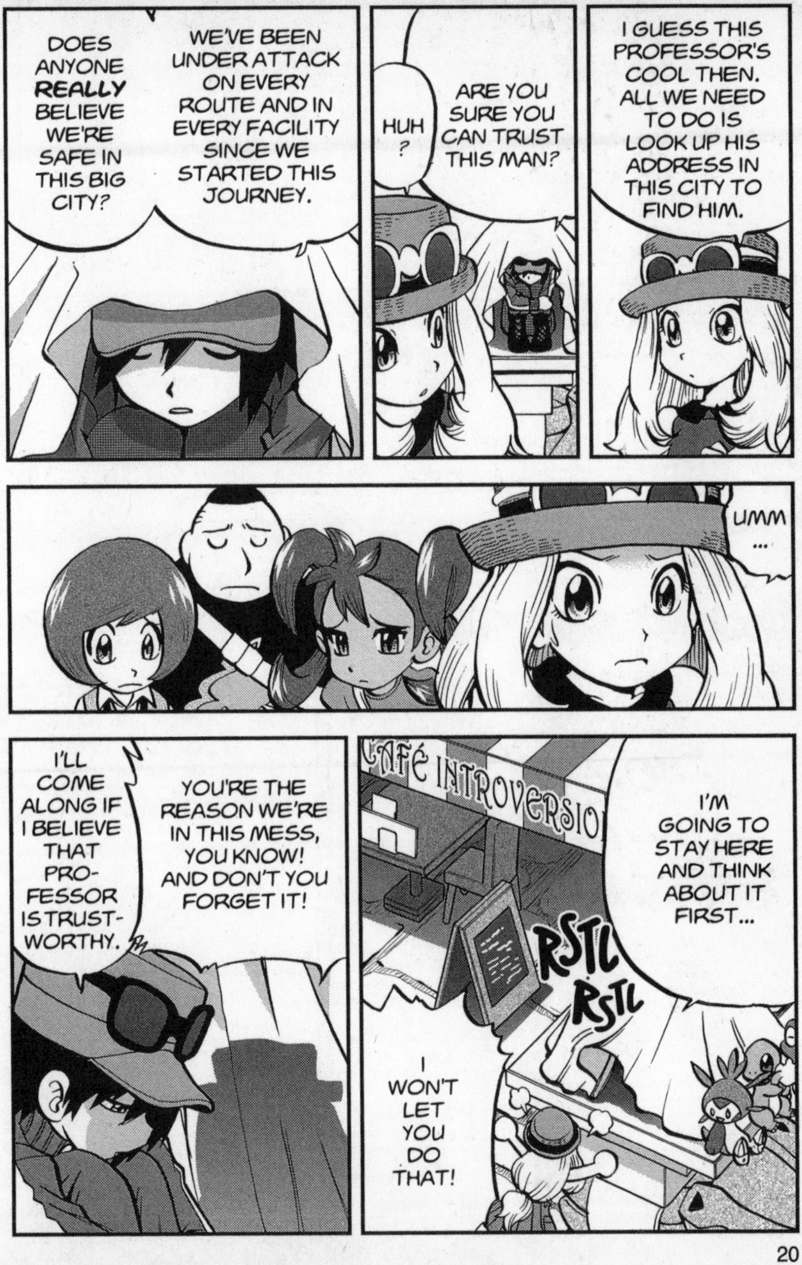
I GUESS THIS PROFESSOR'S COOL THEN. ALL WE NEED TO DO IS LOOK UP HIS ADDRESS IN THIS CITY TO FIND HIM.
ARE YOU SURE YOU CAN TRUST THIS MAN?
HUH ?
WE'VE BEEN UNDER ATTACK ON EVERY ROUTE AND IN EVERY FACILITY SINCE WE STARTED THIS JOURNEY.
DOES ANYONE **REALLY** BELIEVE WE'RE SAFE IN THIS BIG CITY?
UMM ...
I'M GOING TO STAY HERE AND THINK ABOUT IT FIRST...
CAFÉ INTROVERSIO
RSTL
RSTL
I WON'T LET YOU DO THAT!
YOU'RE THE REASON WE'RE IN THIS MESS, YOU KNOW! AND DON'T YOU FORGET IT!
I'LL COME ALONG IF I BELIEVE THAT PRO-FESSOR IS TRUST-WORTHY.

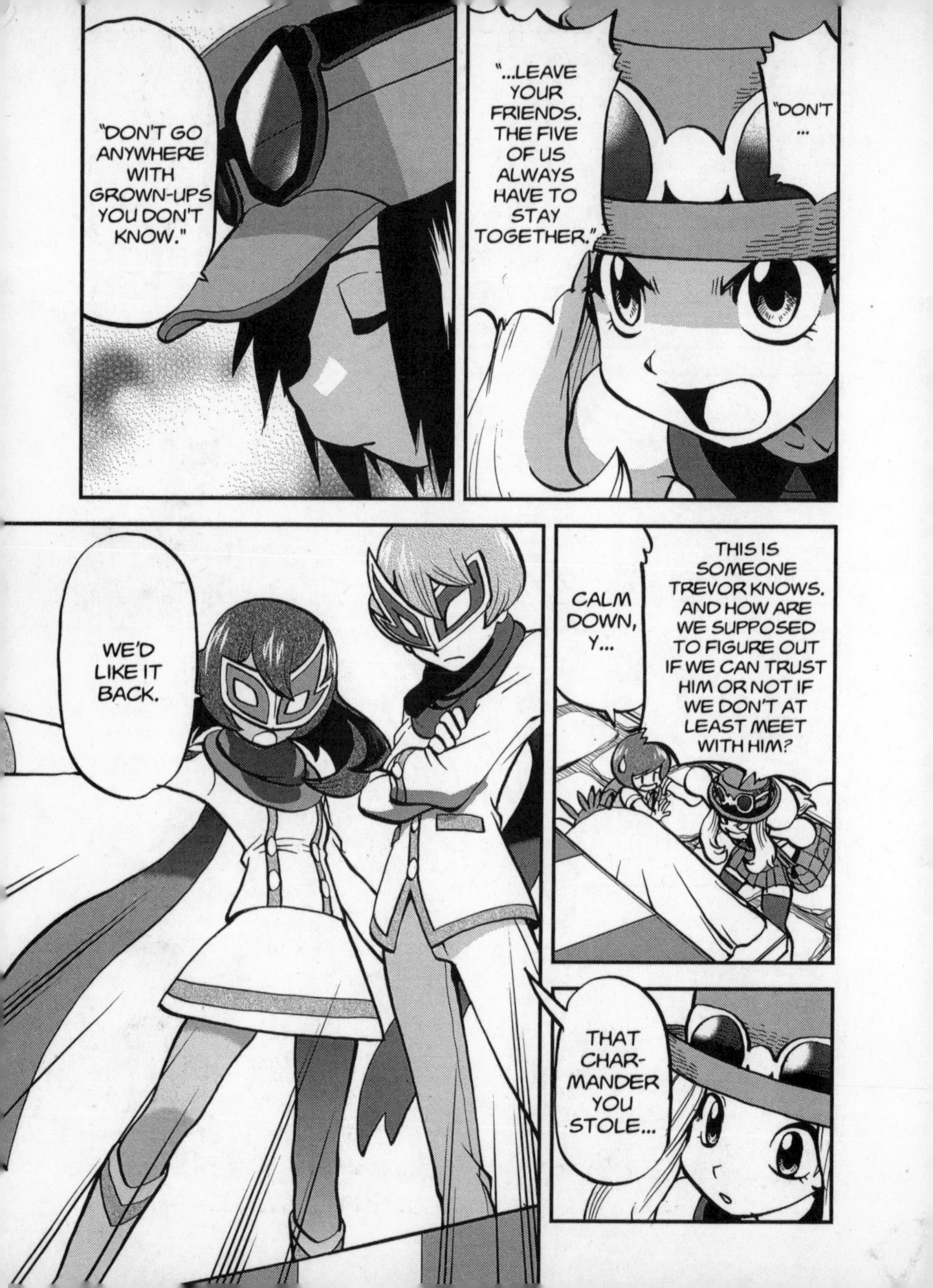
"DON'T ...
"...LEAVE YOUR FRIENDS. THE FIVE OF US ALWAYS HAVE TO STAY TOGETHER."
"DON'T GO ANYWHERE WITH GROWN-UPS YOU DON'T KNOW."
THIS IS SOMEONE TREVOR KNOWS. AND HOW ARE WE SUPPOSED TO FIGURE OUT IF WE CAN TRUST HIM OR NOT IF WE DON'T AT LEAST MEET WITH HIM?
CALM DOWN, Y...
THAT CHAR-MANDER YOU STOLE...
WE'D LIKE IT BACK.

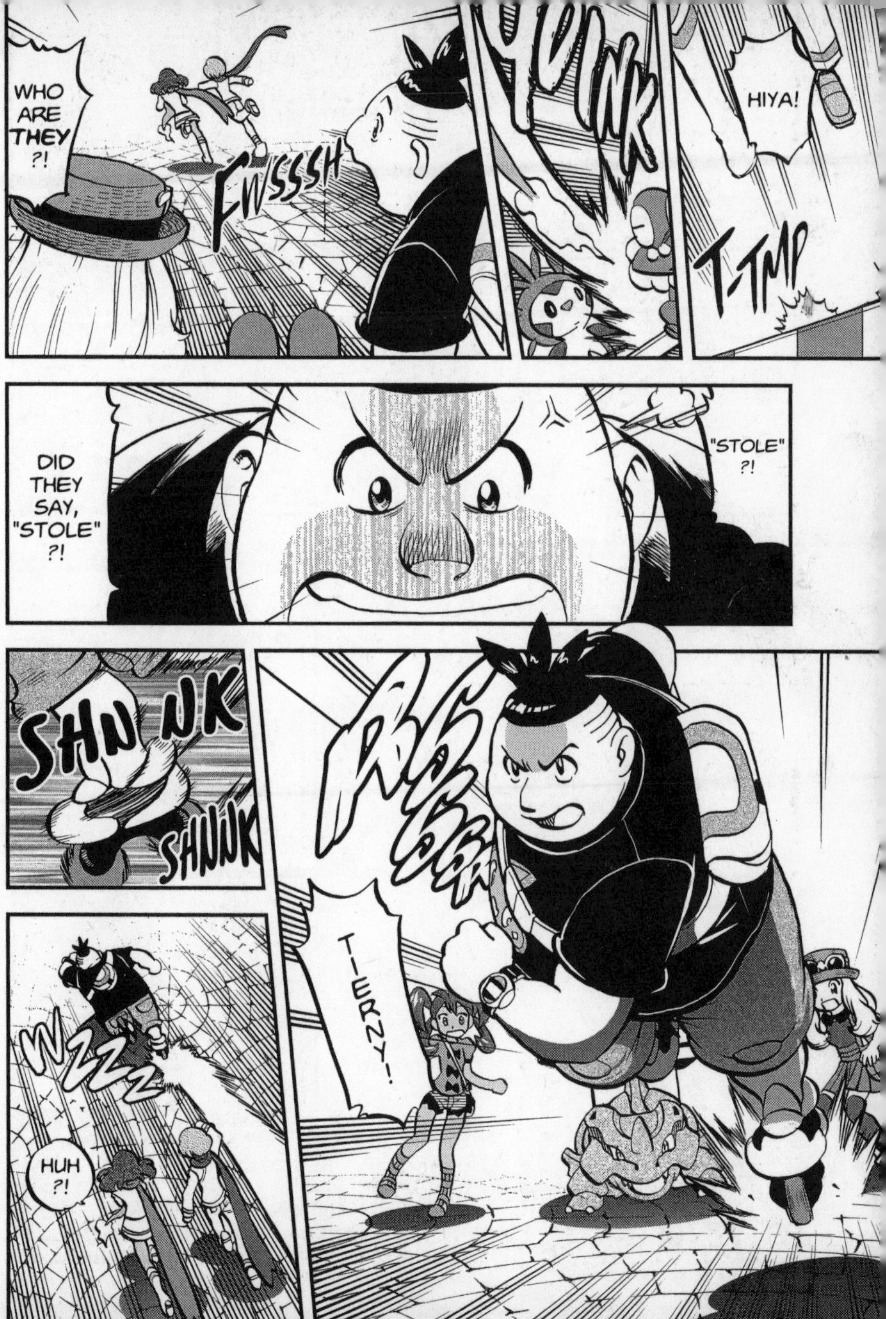
HIYA!
T-TMP
YOINK
WHO ARE THEY ?!
FWSSSH
"STOLE" ?!
DID THEY SAY, "STOLE" ?!
TIERNY!
SHNNK
SHNNK
WZZZ
HUH ?!

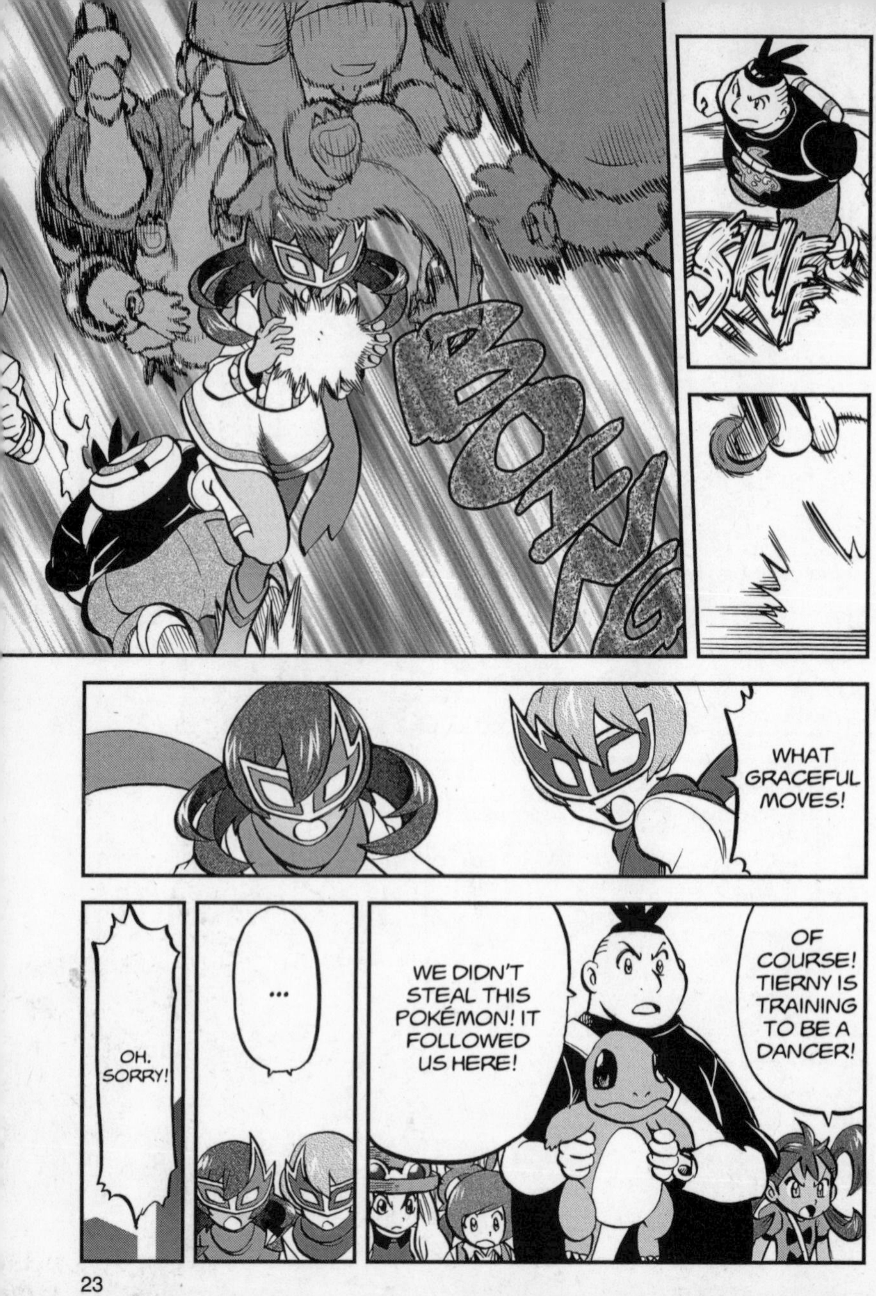
SHF
BOING
WHAT GRACEFUL MOVES!
OF COURSE! TIERNY IS TRAINING TO BE A DANCER!
WE DIDN'T STEAL THIS POKÉMON! IT FOLLOWED US HERE!
...
OH. SORRY!

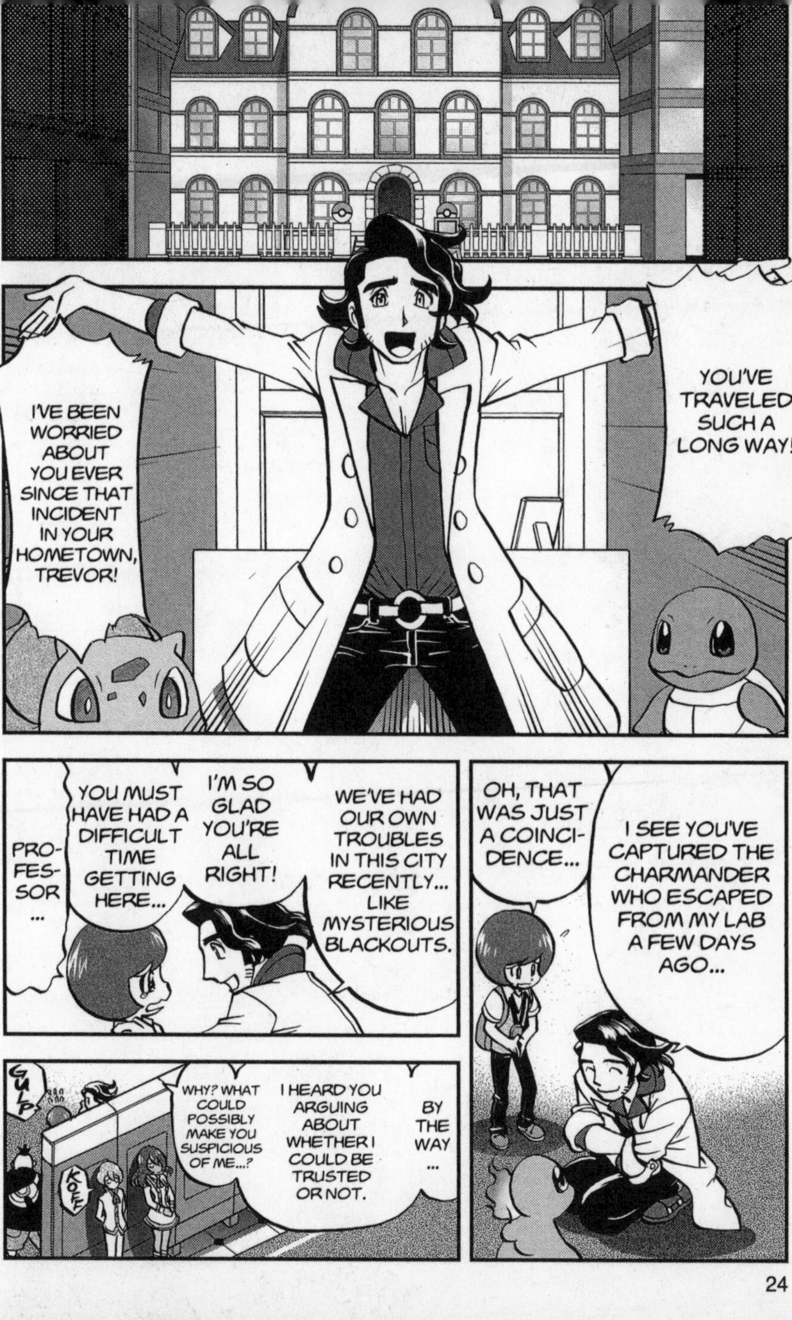
YOU'VE TRAVELED SUCH A LONG WAY!
I'VE BEEN WORRIED ABOUT YOU EVER SINCE THAT INCIDENT IN YOUR HOMETOWN, TREVOR!
I SEE YOU'VE CAPTURED THE CHARMANDER WHO ESCAPED FROM MY LAB A FEW DAYS AGO...
OH, THAT WAS JUST A COINCIDENCE...
WE'VE HAD OUR OWN TROUBLES IN THIS CITY RECENTLY... LIKE MYSTERIOUS BLACKOUTS.
I'M SO GLAD YOU'RE ALL RIGHT!
YOU MUST HAVE HAD A DIFFICULT TIME GETTING HERE...
PROFESSOR...
BY THE WAY...
I HEARD YOU ARGUING ABOUT WHETHER I COULD BE TRUSTED OR NOT.
WHY? WHAT COULD POSSIBLY MAKE YOU SUSPICIOUS OF ME...?
KOFF
GULP

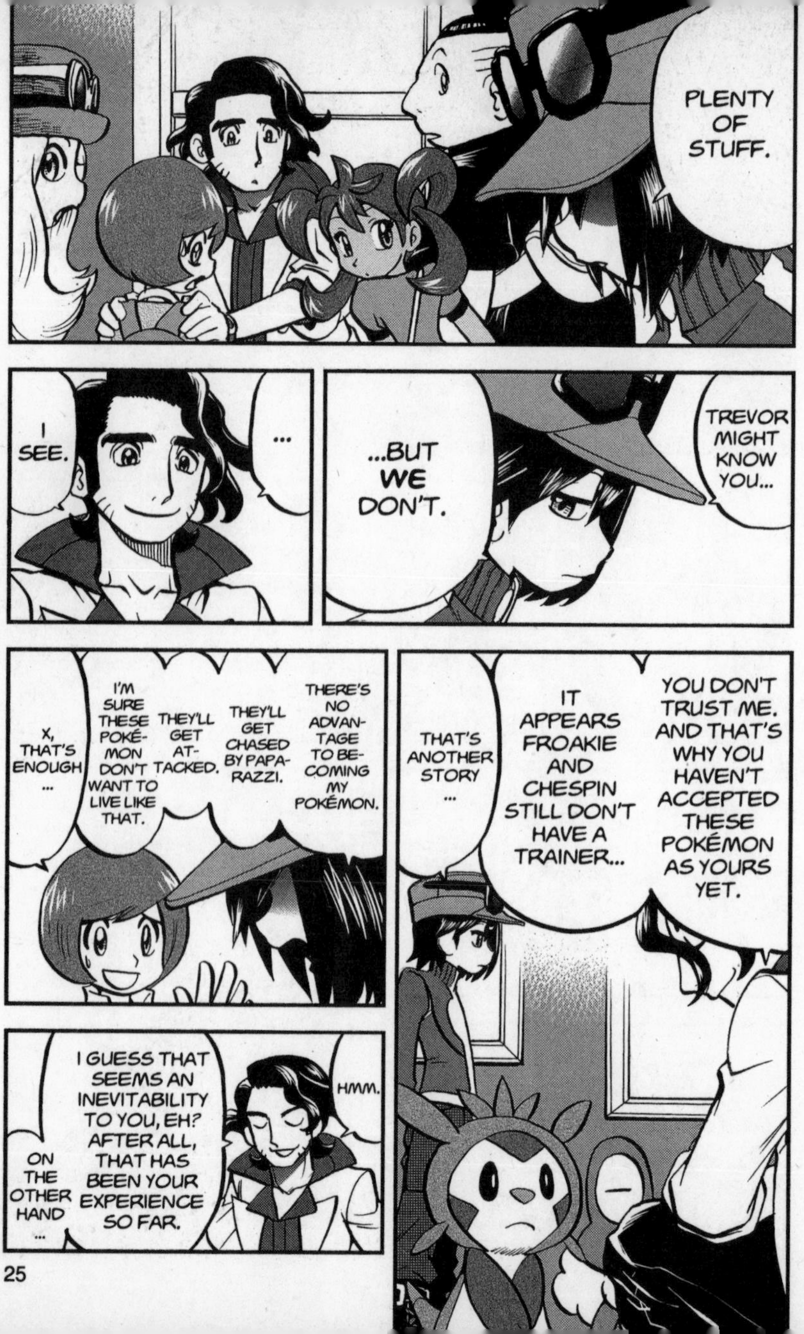
PLENTY OF STUFF.
TREVOR MIGHT KNOW YOU...
...BUT WE DON'T.
...
I SEE.
YOU DON'T TRUST ME. AND THAT'S WHY YOU HAVEN'T ACCEPTED THESE POKÉMON AS YOURS YET.
IT APPEARS FROAKIE AND CHESPIN STILL DON'T HAVE A TRAINER...
THAT'S ANOTHER STORY ...
THERE'S NO ADVAN-TAGE TO BE-COMING MY POKÉMON.
THEY'LL GET CHASED BY PAPA-RAZZI.
THEY'LL GET AT-TACKED.
I'M SURE THESE POKÉ-MON DON'T WANT TO LIVE LIKE THAT.
X, THAT'S ENOUGH ...
HMM.
I GUESS THAT SEEMS AN INEVITABILITY TO YOU, EH? AFTER ALL, THAT HAS BEEN YOUR EXPERIENCE SO FAR.
ON THE OTHER HAND ...

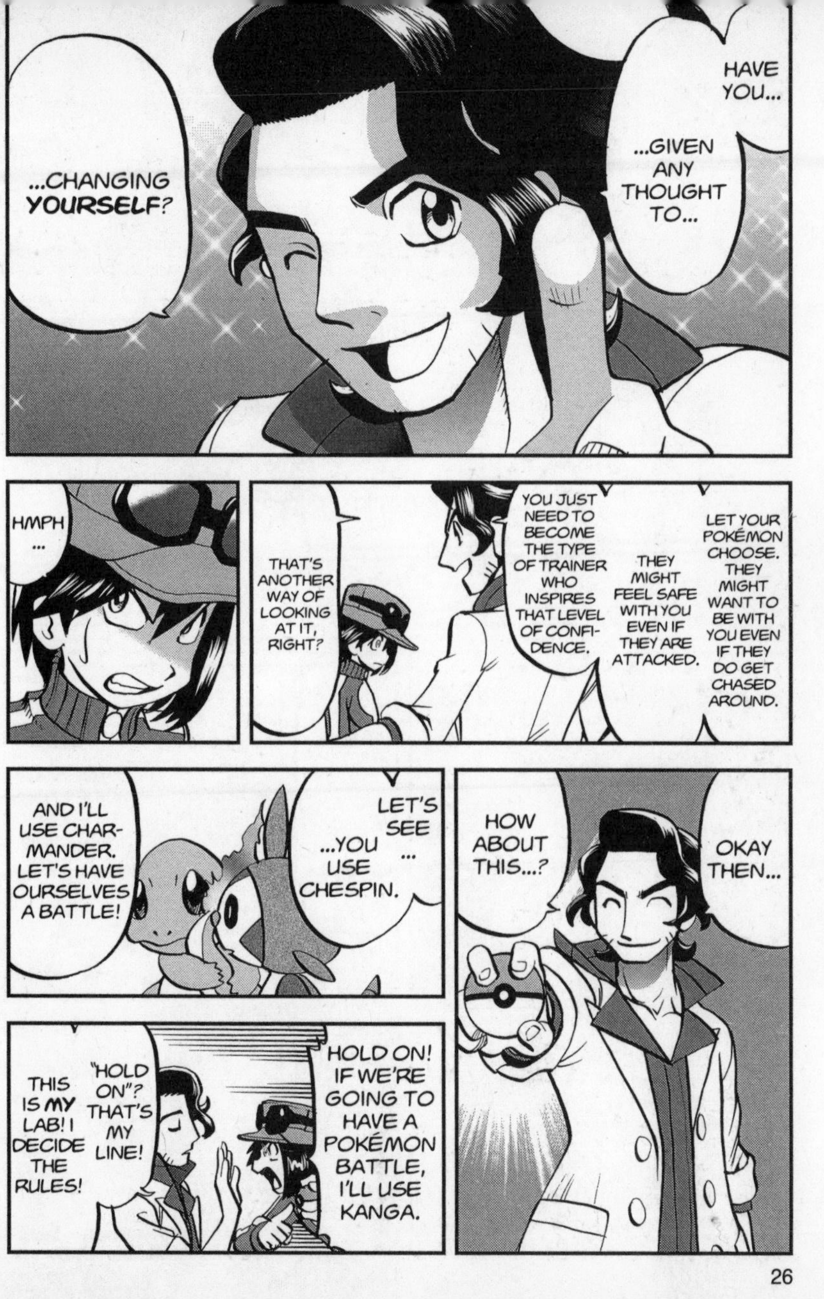
HAVE YOU...
...GIVEN ANY THOUGHT TO...
...CHANGING **YOURSELF**?
LET YOUR POKÉMON CHOOSE. THEY MIGHT WANT TO BE WITH YOU EVEN IF THEY DO GET CHASED AROUND.
THEY MIGHT FEEL SAFE WITH YOU EVEN IF THEY ARE ATTACKED.
YOU JUST NEED TO BECOME THE TYPE OF TRAINER WHO INSPIRES THAT LEVEL OF CONFI-DENCE.
THAT'S ANOTHER WAY OF LOOKING AT IT, RIGHT?
HMPH...
OKAY THEN...
HOW ABOUT THIS...?
LET'S SEE...
...YOU USE CHESPIN.
AND I'LL USE CHAR-MANDER. LET'S HAVE OURSELVES A BATTLE!
HOLD ON! IF WE'RE GOING TO HAVE A POKÉMON BATTLE, I'LL USE KANGA.
"HOLD ON"? THAT'S MY LINE!
THIS IS **MY** LAB! I DECIDE THE RULES!

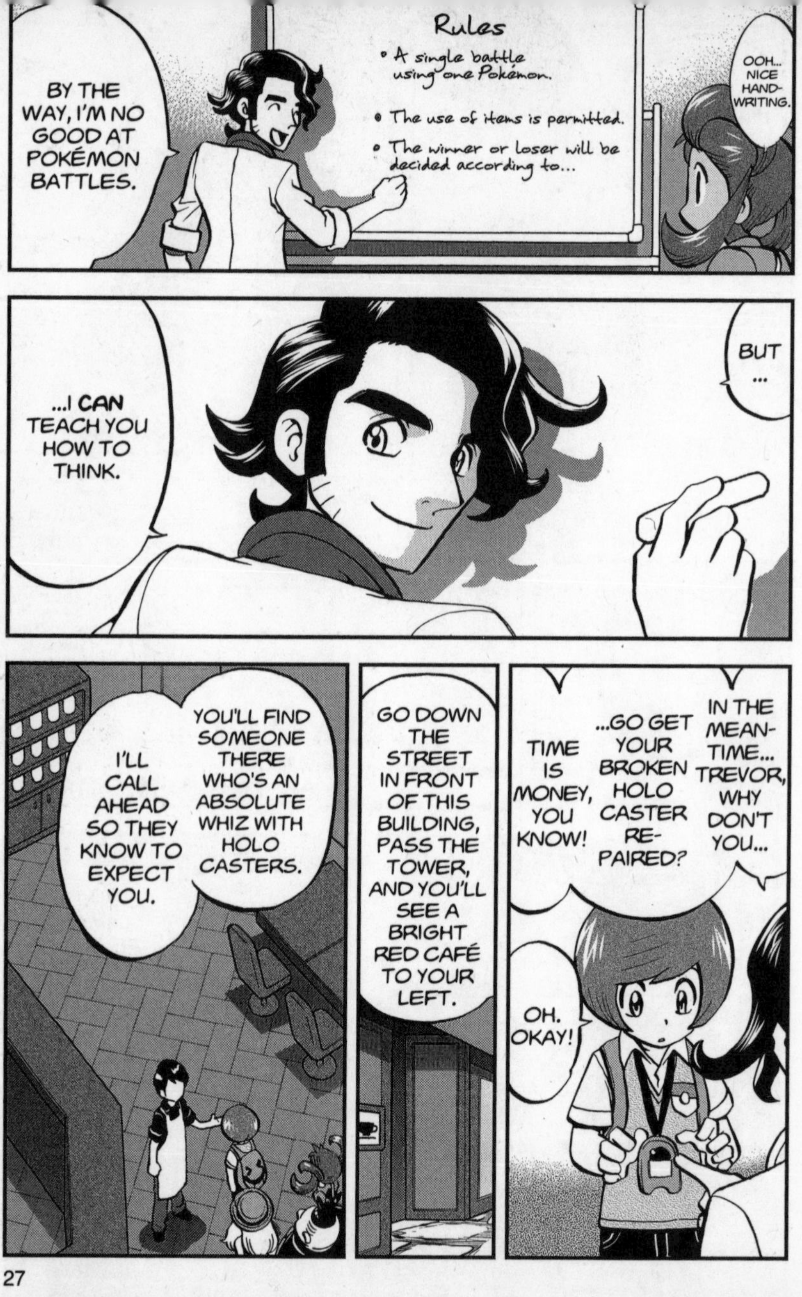
OOH... NICE HAND-WRITING.
Rules
• A single battle using one Pokémon.
• The use of items is permitted.
• The winner or loser will be decided according to...
BY THE WAY, I'M NO GOOD AT POKÉMON BATTLES.
BUT ...
...I CAN TEACH YOU HOW TO THINK.
IN THE MEAN-TIME... TREVOR, WHY DON'T YOU...
...GO GET YOUR BROKEN HOLO CASTER RE-PAIRED?
TIME IS MONEY, YOU KNOW!
OH. OKAY!
GO DOWN THE STREET IN FRONT OF THIS BUILDING, PASS THE TOWER, AND YOU'LL SEE A BRIGHT RED CAFÉ TO YOUR LEFT.
YOU'LL FIND SOMEONE THERE WHO'S AN ABSOLUTE WHIZ WITH HOLO CASTERS.
I'LL CALL AHEAD SO THEY KNOW TO EXPECT YOU.

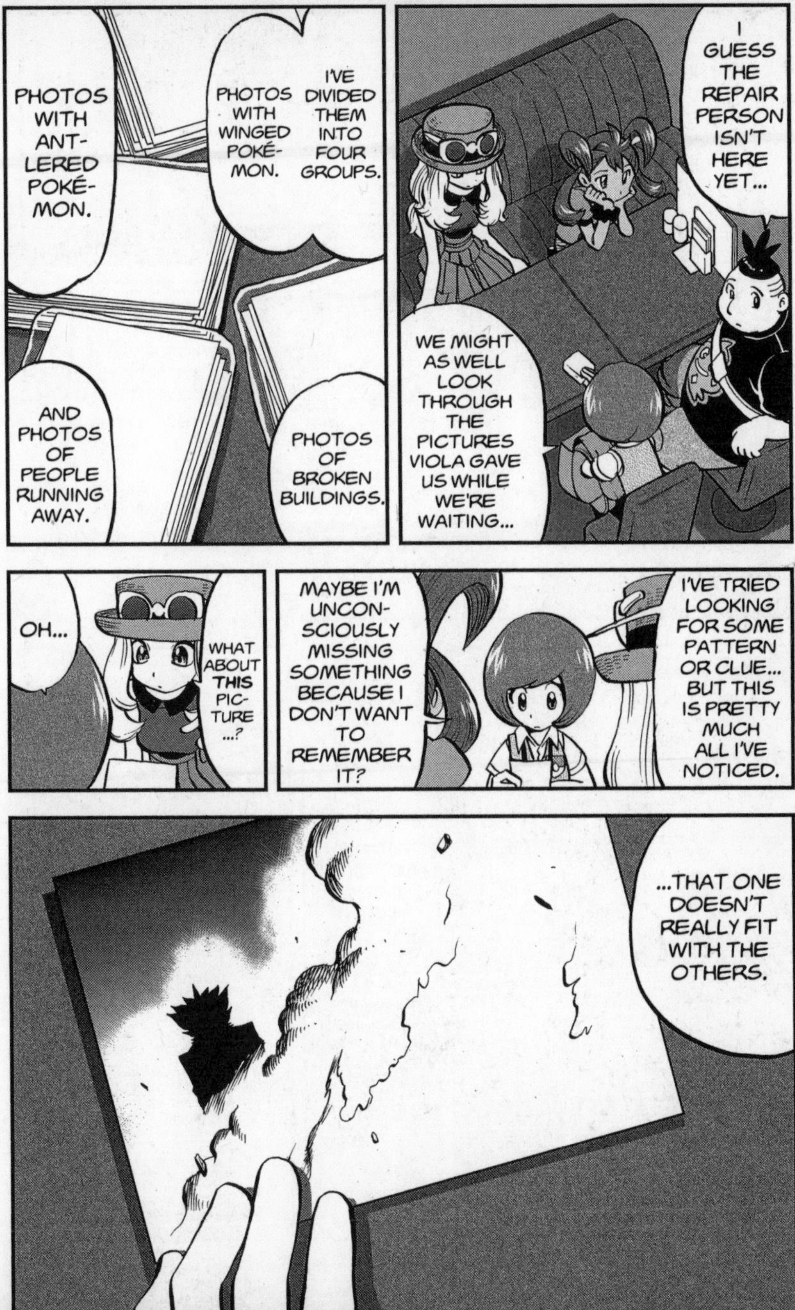
I GUESS THE REPAIR PERSON ISN'T HERE YET...
WE MIGHT AS WELL LOOK THROUGH THE PICTURES VIOLA GAVE US WHILE WE'RE WAITING...
I'VE DIVIDED THEM INTO FOUR GROUPS.
PHOTOS WITH WINGED POKÉMON.
PHOTOS WITH ANTLERED POKÉMON.
PHOTOS OF BROKEN BUILDINGS.
AND PHOTOS OF PEOPLE RUNNING AWAY.
I'VE TRIED LOOKING FOR SOME PATTERN OR CLUE... BUT THIS IS PRETTY MUCH ALL I'VE NOTICED.
MAYBE I'M UNCONSCIOUSLY MISSING SOMETHING BECAUSE I DON'T WANT TO REMEMBER IT?
WHAT ABOUT **THIS** PICTURE...?
OH...
...THAT ONE DOESN'T REALLY FIT WITH THE OTHERS.

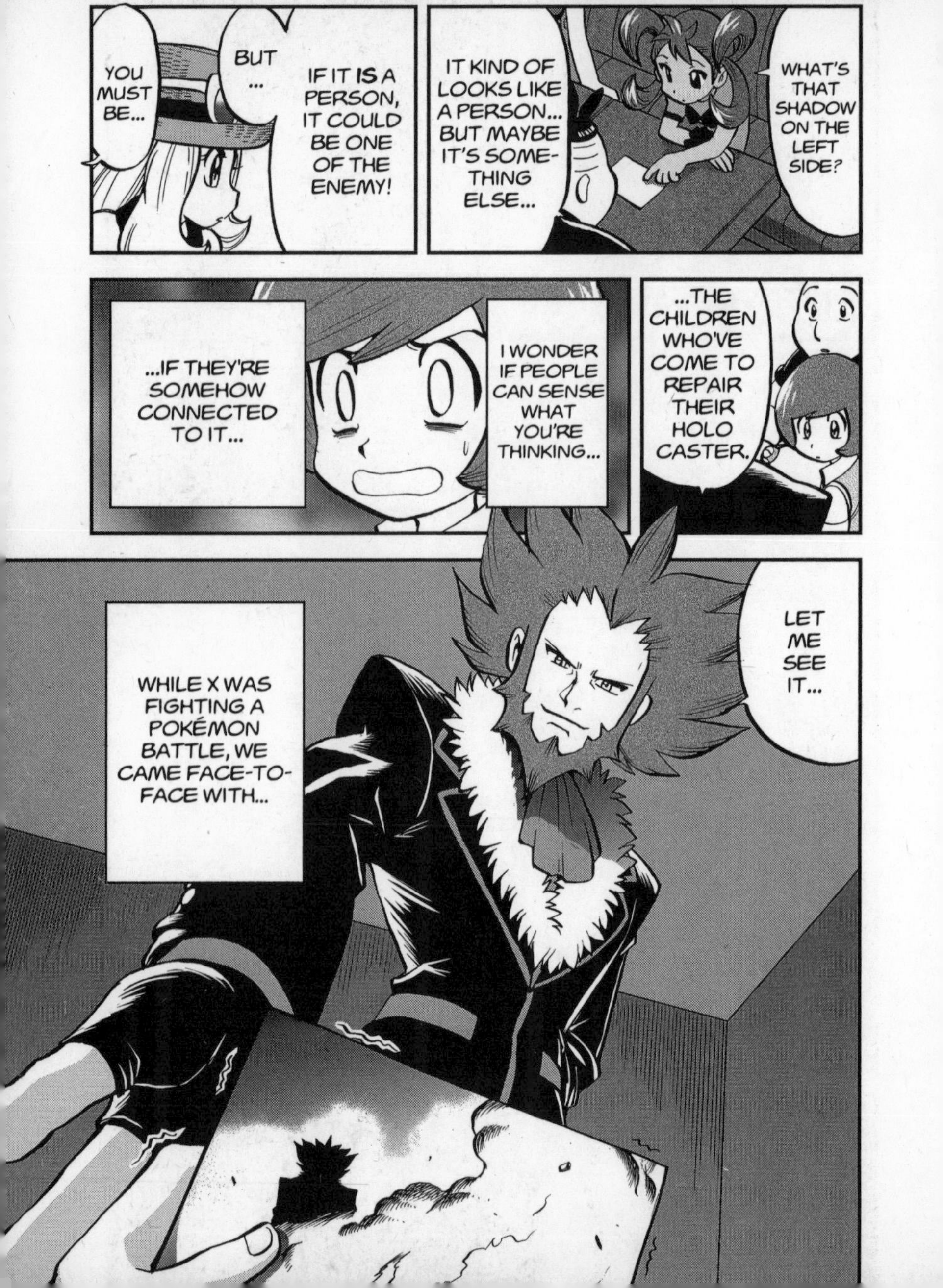
WHAT'S THAT SHADOW ON THE LEFT SIDE?
IT KIND OF LOOKS LIKE A PERSON... BUT MAYBE IT'S SOME-THING ELSE...
IF IT **IS** A PERSON, IT COULD BE ONE OF THE ENEMY!
BUT ...
YOU MUST BE...
...THE CHILDREN WHO'VE COME TO REPAIR THEIR HOLO CASTER.
I WONDER IF PEOPLE CAN SENSE WHAT YOU'RE THINKING...
...IF THEY'RE SOMEHOW CONNECTED TO IT...
LET ME SEE IT...
WHILE X WAS FIGHTING A POKÉMON BATTLE, WE CAME FACE-TO-FACE WITH...

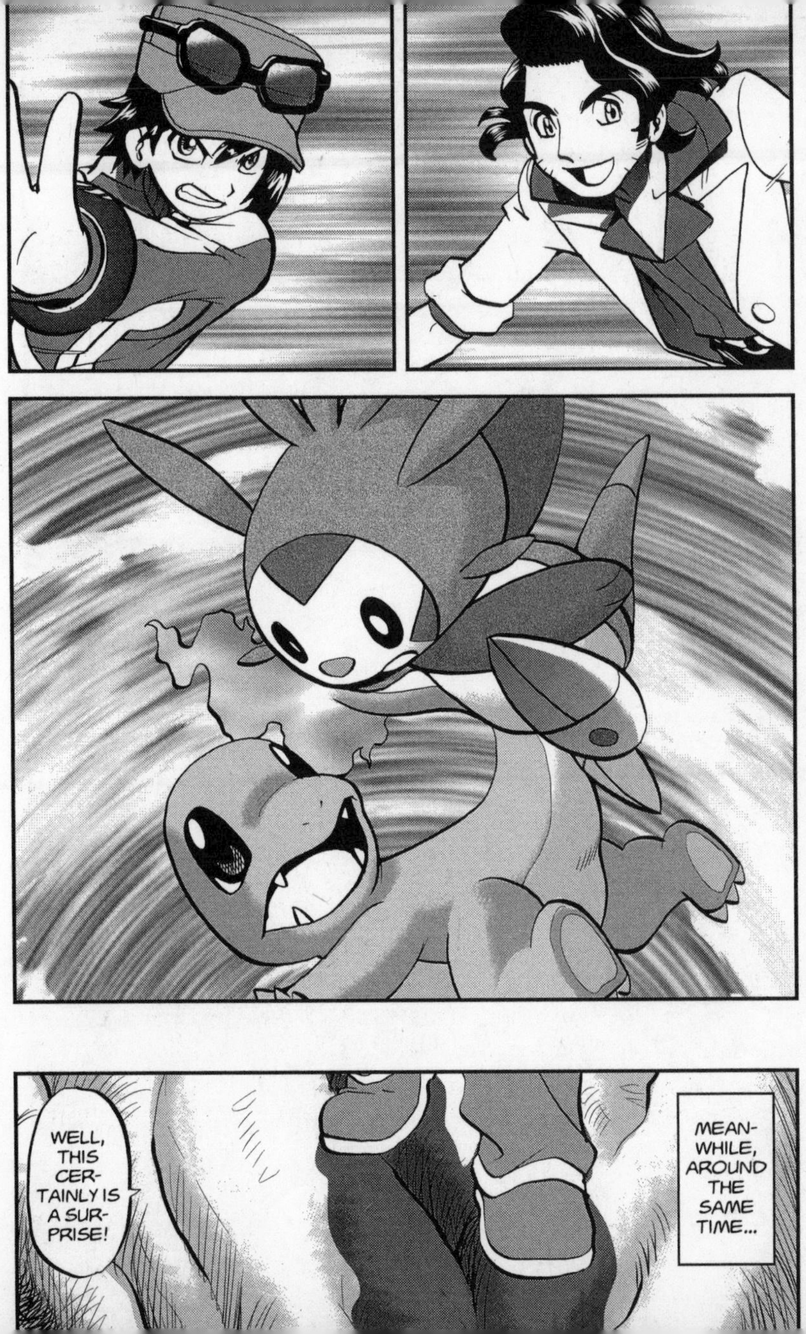
MEAN-WHILE, AROUND THE SAME TIME...
WELL, THIS CER-TAINLY IS A SUR-PRISE!

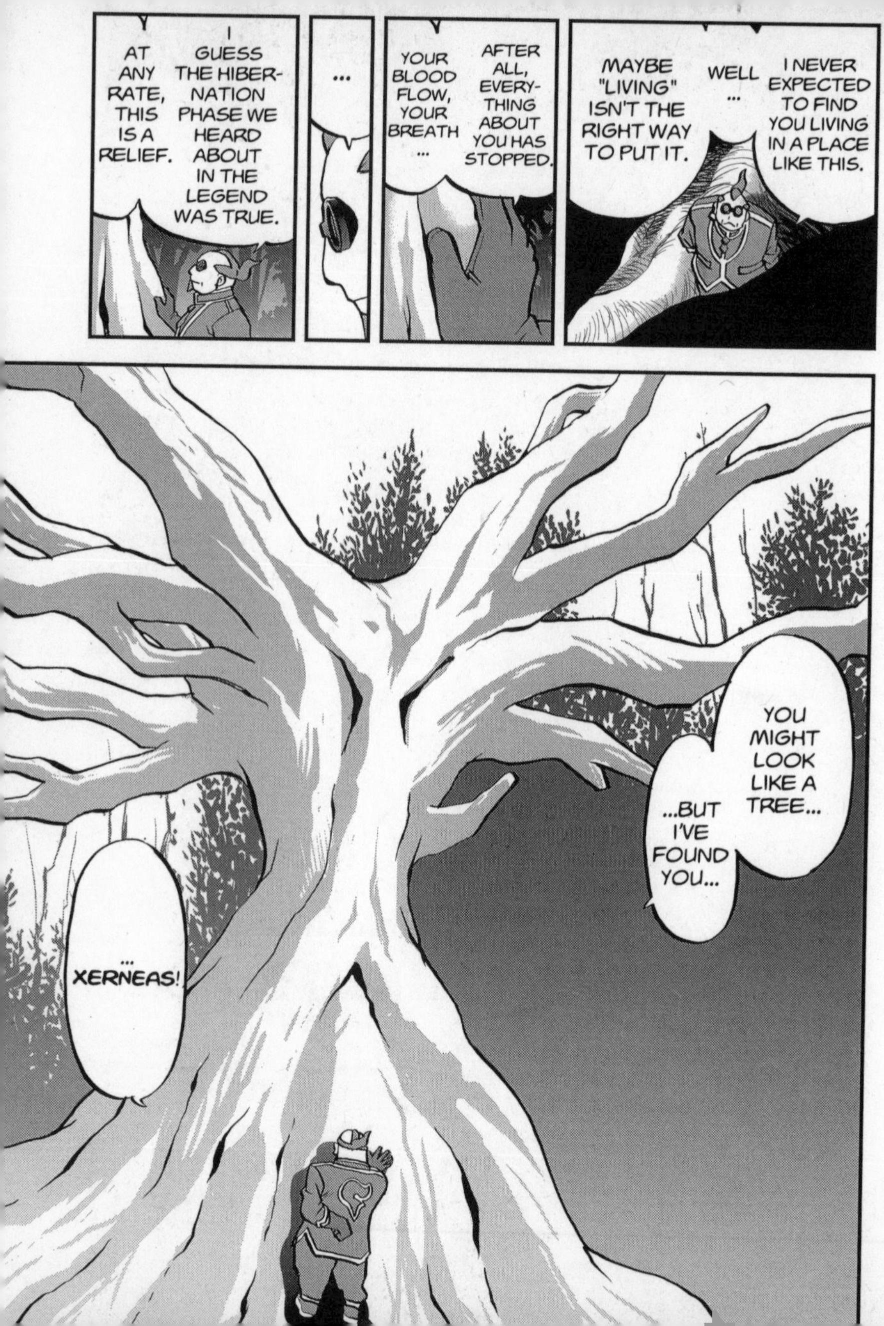
I NEVER EXPECTED TO FIND YOU LIVING IN A PLACE LIKE THIS.
WELL ...
MAYBE "LIVING" ISN'T THE RIGHT WAY TO PUT IT.
AFTER ALL, EVERYTHING ABOUT YOU HAS STOPPED.
YOUR BLOOD FLOW, YOUR BREATH ...
...
I GUESS THE HIBERNATION PHASE WE HEARD ABOUT IN THE LEGEND WAS TRUE.
AT ANY RATE, THIS IS A RELIEF.
YOU MIGHT LOOK LIKE A TREE...
...BUT I'VE FOUND YOU...
... XERNEAS!

## Current Location

**Route 4**
**Parterre Way**

This famed path's perfectly designed
and executed gardens are its highlight
and a special point of pride.

**Lumiose City**

A dazzling metropolis of art and
artifice, located in the very heart of
the Kalos region.

# Adventure 9 Chespin Sows the Seeds of Change

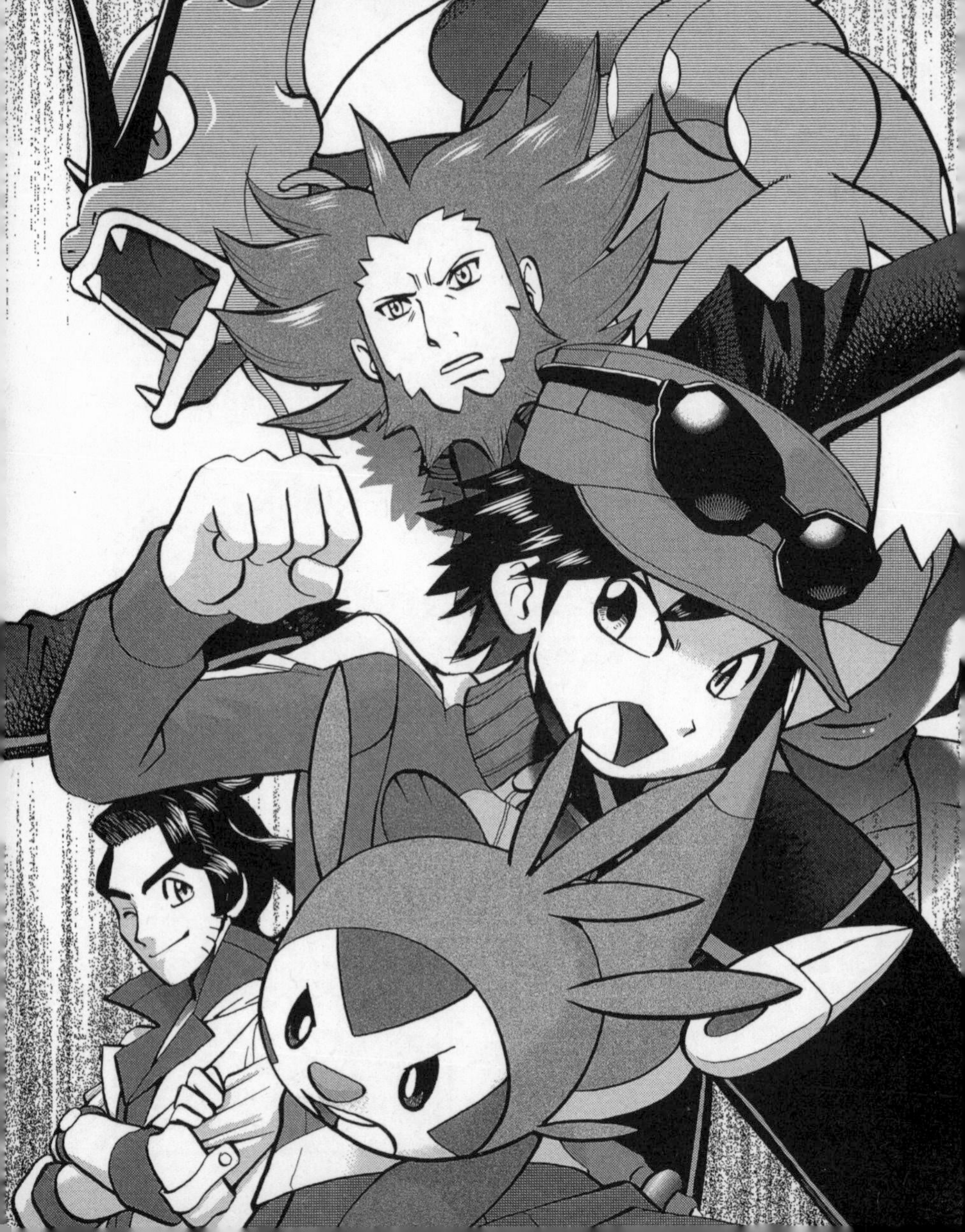

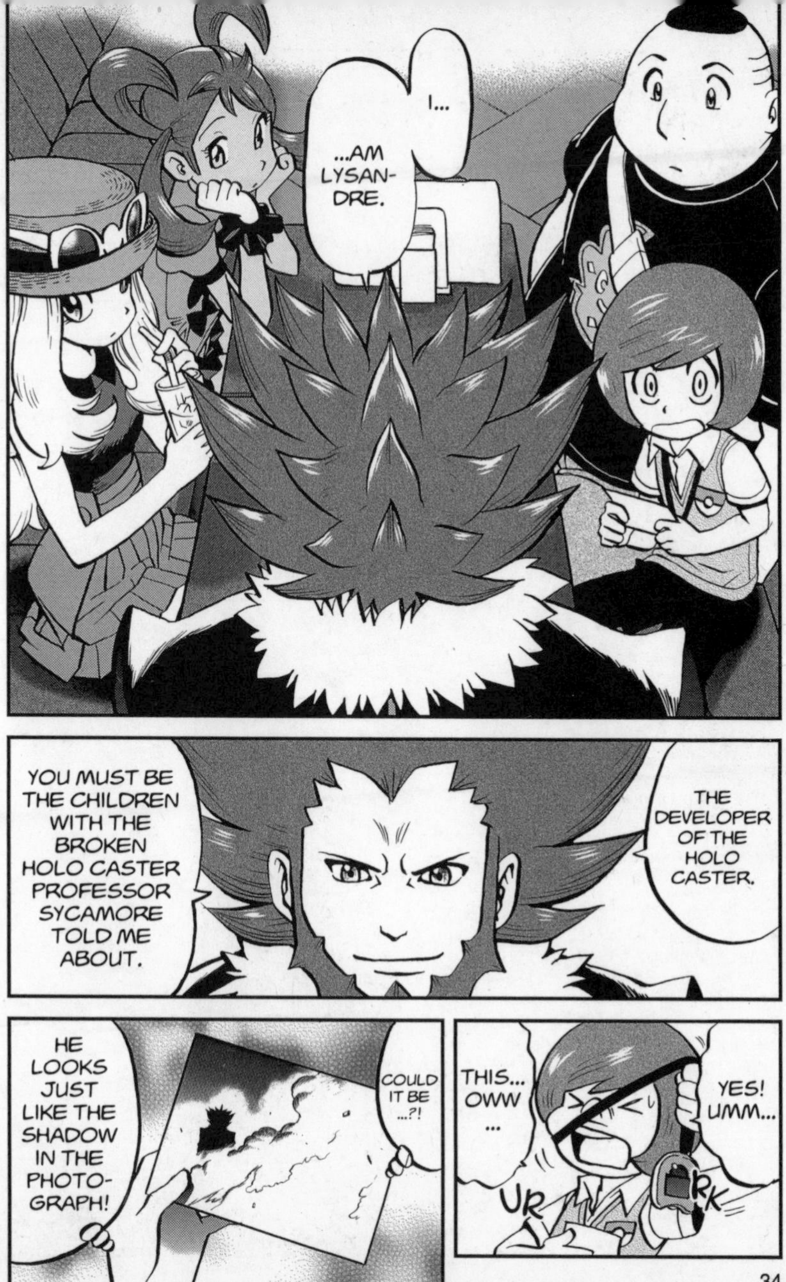
I...
...AM LYSANDRE.
THE DEVELOPER OF THE HOLO CASTER.
YOU MUST BE THE CHILDREN WITH THE BROKEN HOLO CASTER PROFESSOR SYCAMORE TOLD ME ABOUT.
YES! UMM...
THIS... OWW ...
URRK
COULD IT BE ...?!
HE LOOKS JUST LIKE THE SHADOW IN THE PHOTOGRAPH!

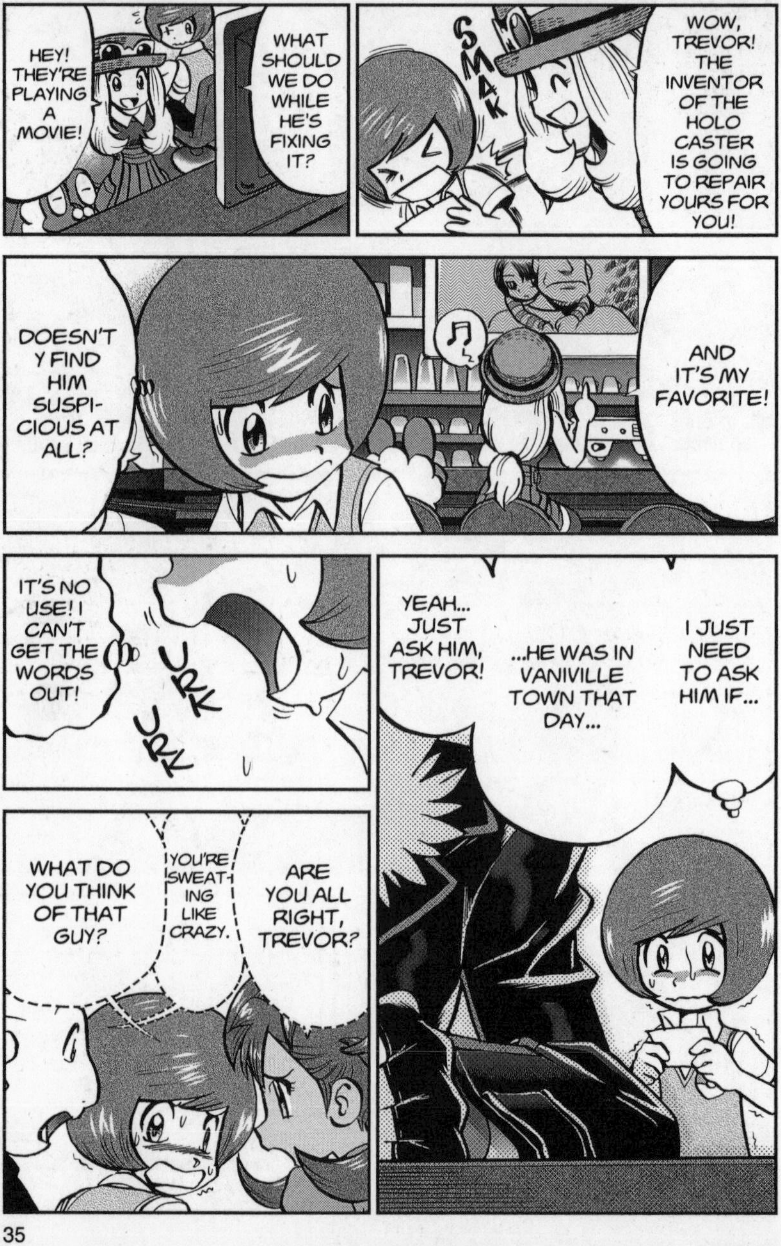
WOW, TREVOR! THE INVENTOR OF THE HOLO CASTER IS GOING TO REPAIR YOURS FOR YOU!
SMAK
WHAT SHOULD WE DO WHILE HE'S FIXING IT?
HEY! THEY'RE PLAYING A MOVIE!
AND IT'S MY FAVORITE!
DOESN'T Y FIND HIM SUSPI-CIOUS AT ALL?
I JUST NEED TO ASK HIM IF...
...HE WAS IN VANIVILLE TOWN THAT DAY...
YEAH... JUST ASK HIM, TREVOR!
IT'S NO USE! I CAN'T GET THE WORDS OUT!
URK URK
ARE YOU ALL RIGHT, TREVOR?
YOU'RE SWEAT-ING LIKE CRAZY.
WHAT DO YOU THINK OF THAT GUY?

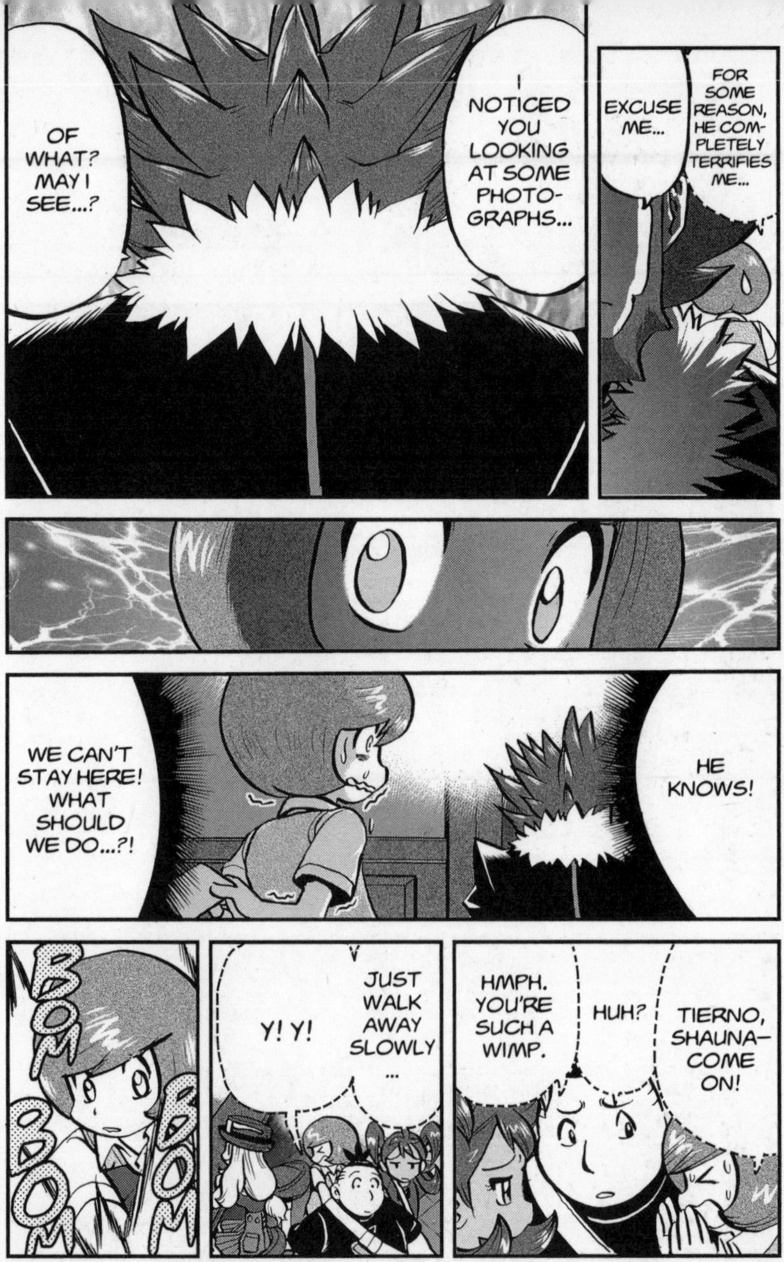
FOR SOME REASON, HE COMPLETELY TERRIFIES ME...
EXCUSE ME...
I NOTICED YOU LOOKING AT SOME PHOTOGRAPHS...
OF WHAT? MAY I SEE...?
HE KNOWS!
WE CAN'T STAY HERE! WHAT SHOULD WE DO...?!
TIERNO, SHAUNA—COME ON!
HUH?
HMPH. YOU'RE SUCH A WIMP.
JUST WALK AWAY SLOWLY...
Y! Y!
BOM BOM
BOOM
BOOM

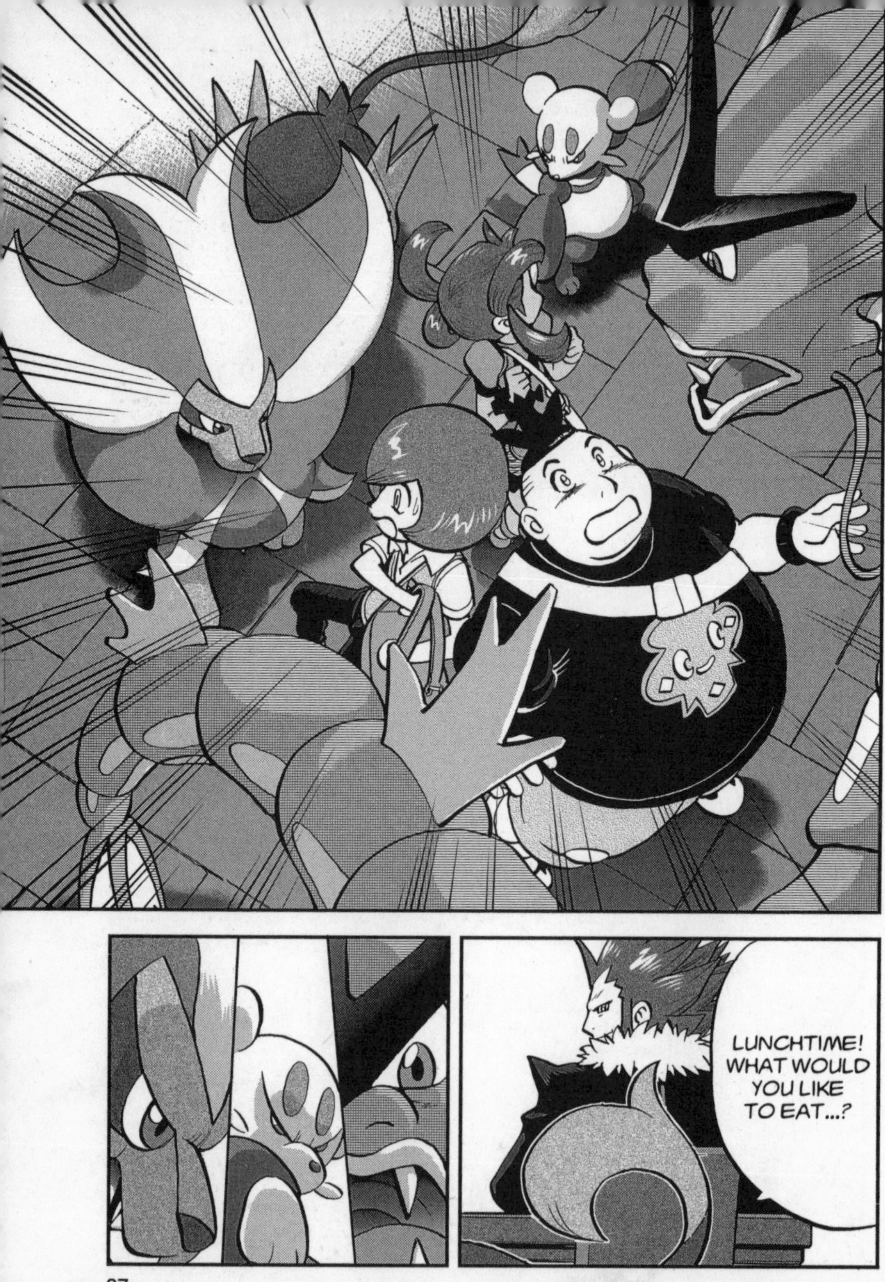
LUNCHTIME! WHAT WOULD YOU LIKE TO EAT...?

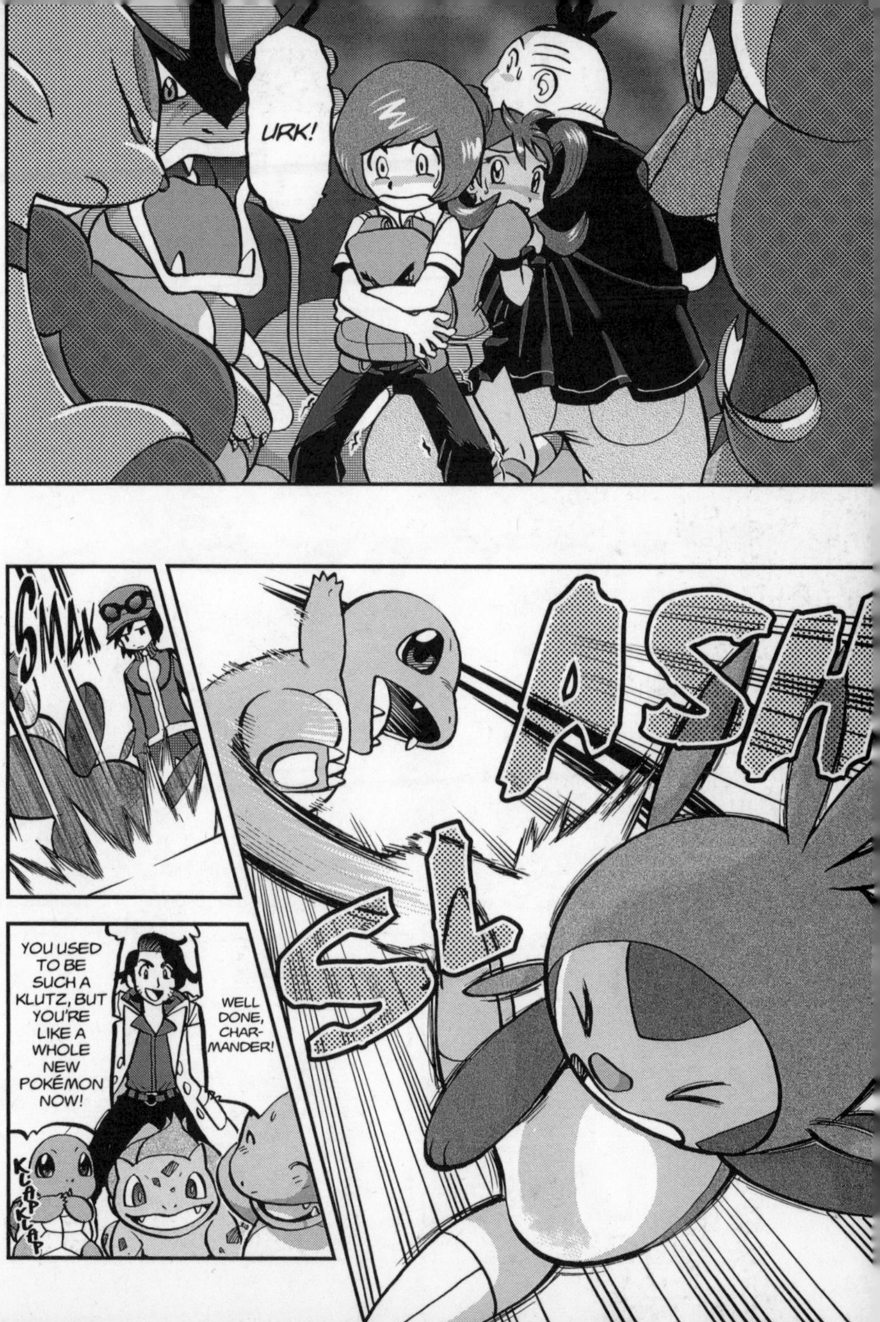
URK!
SLASH
SMAK
WELL DONE, CHARMANDER!
YOU USED TO BE SUCH A KLUTZ, BUT YOU'RE LIKE A WHOLE NEW POKÉMON NOW!
KLAP KLAP

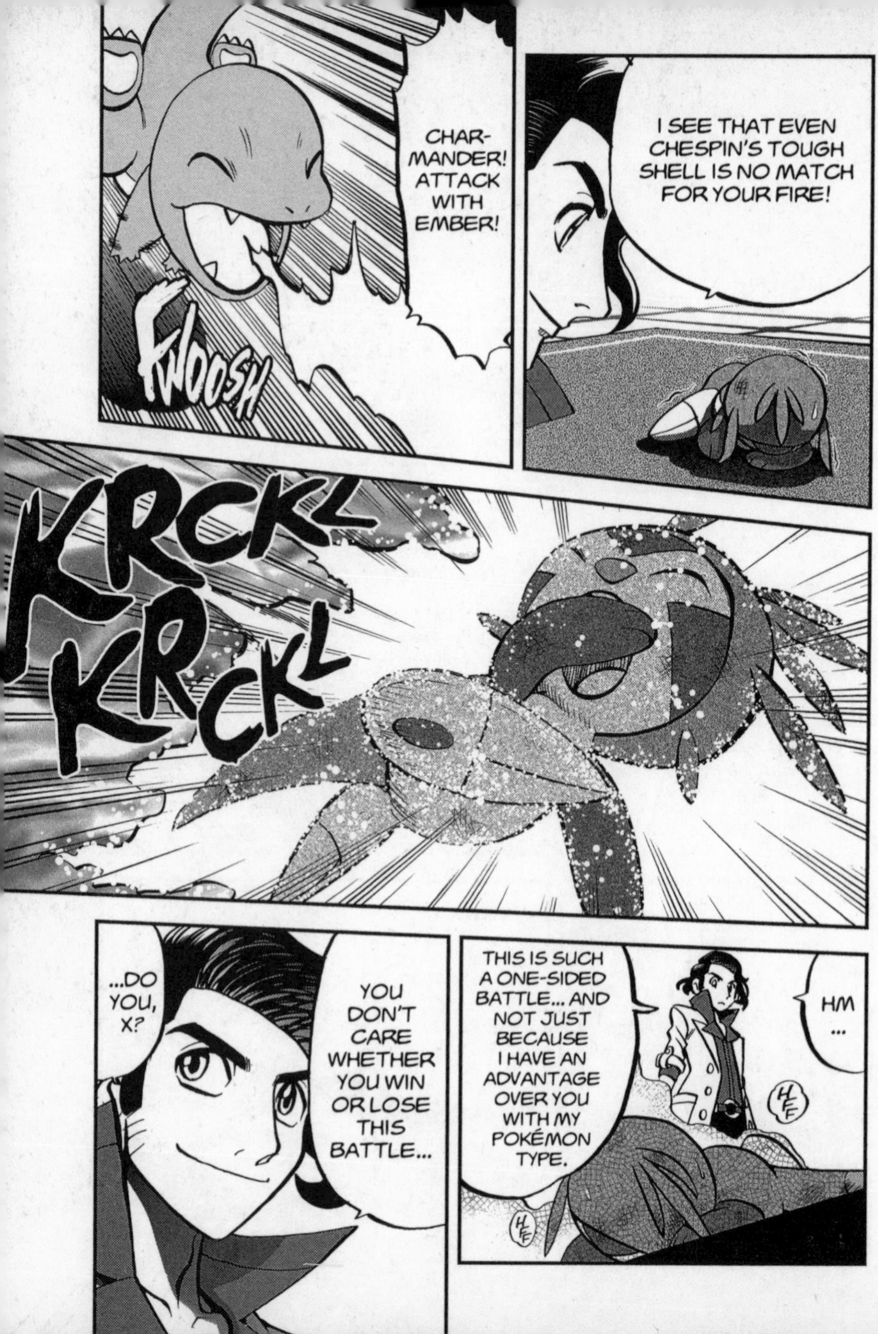
I SEE THAT EVEN CHESPIN'S TOUGH SHELL IS NO MATCH FOR YOUR FIRE!
CHAR-MANDER! ATTACK WITH EMBER!
FWOOSH
KRCKL KRCKL
HM ...
THIS IS SUCH A ONE-SIDED BATTLE... AND NOT JUST BECAUSE I HAVE AN ADVANTAGE OVER YOU WITH MY POKÉMON TYPE.
HFF
HFF
YOU DON'T CARE WHETHER YOU WIN OR LOSE THIS BATTLE...
...DO YOU, X?

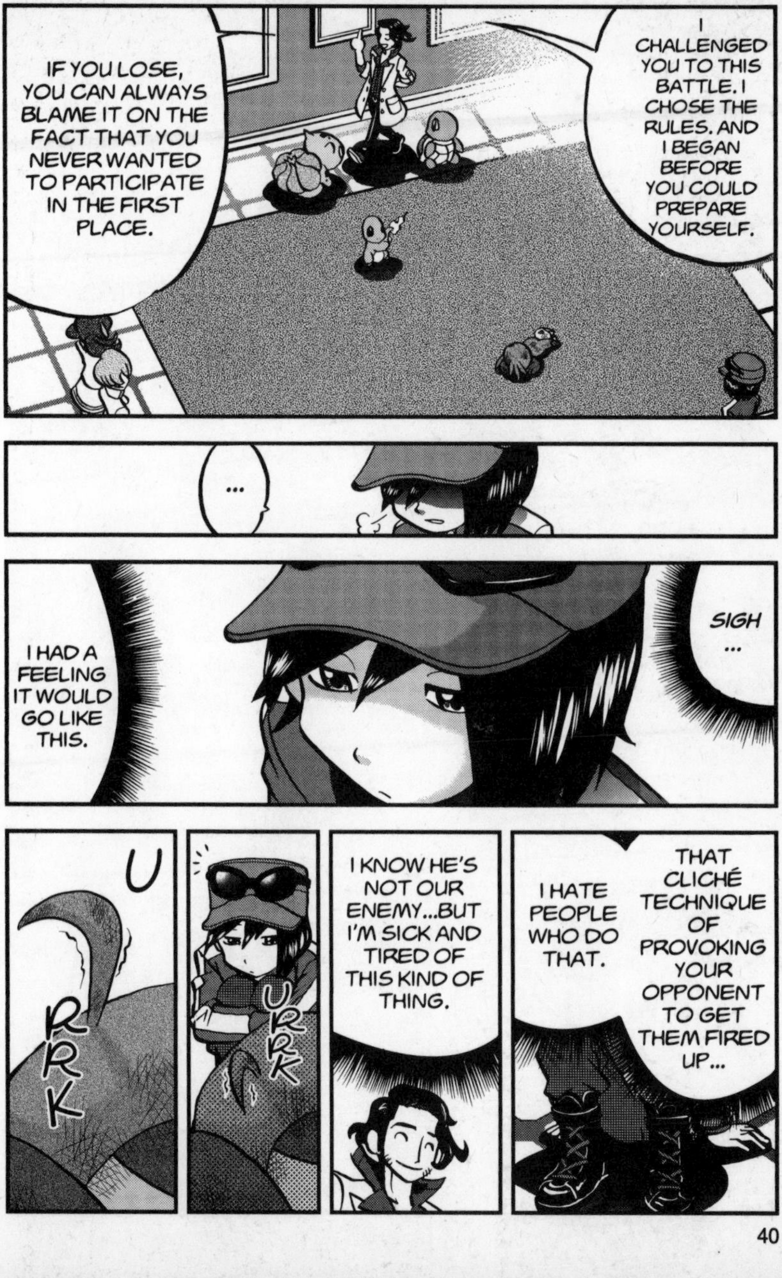
I CHALLENGED YOU TO THIS BATTLE. I CHOSE THE RULES. AND I BEGAN BEFORE YOU COULD PREPARE YOURSELF.
IF YOU LOSE, YOU CAN ALWAYS BLAME IT ON THE FACT THAT YOU NEVER WANTED TO PARTICIPATE IN THE FIRST PLACE.
...
SIGH ...
I HAD A FEELING IT WOULD GO LIKE THIS.
THAT CLICHÉ TECHNIQUE OF PROVOKING YOUR OPPONENT TO GET THEM FIRED UP...
I HATE PEOPLE WHO DO THAT.
I KNOW HE'S NOT OUR ENEMY...BUT I'M SICK AND TIRED OF THIS KIND OF THING.
URRK
U
RRK

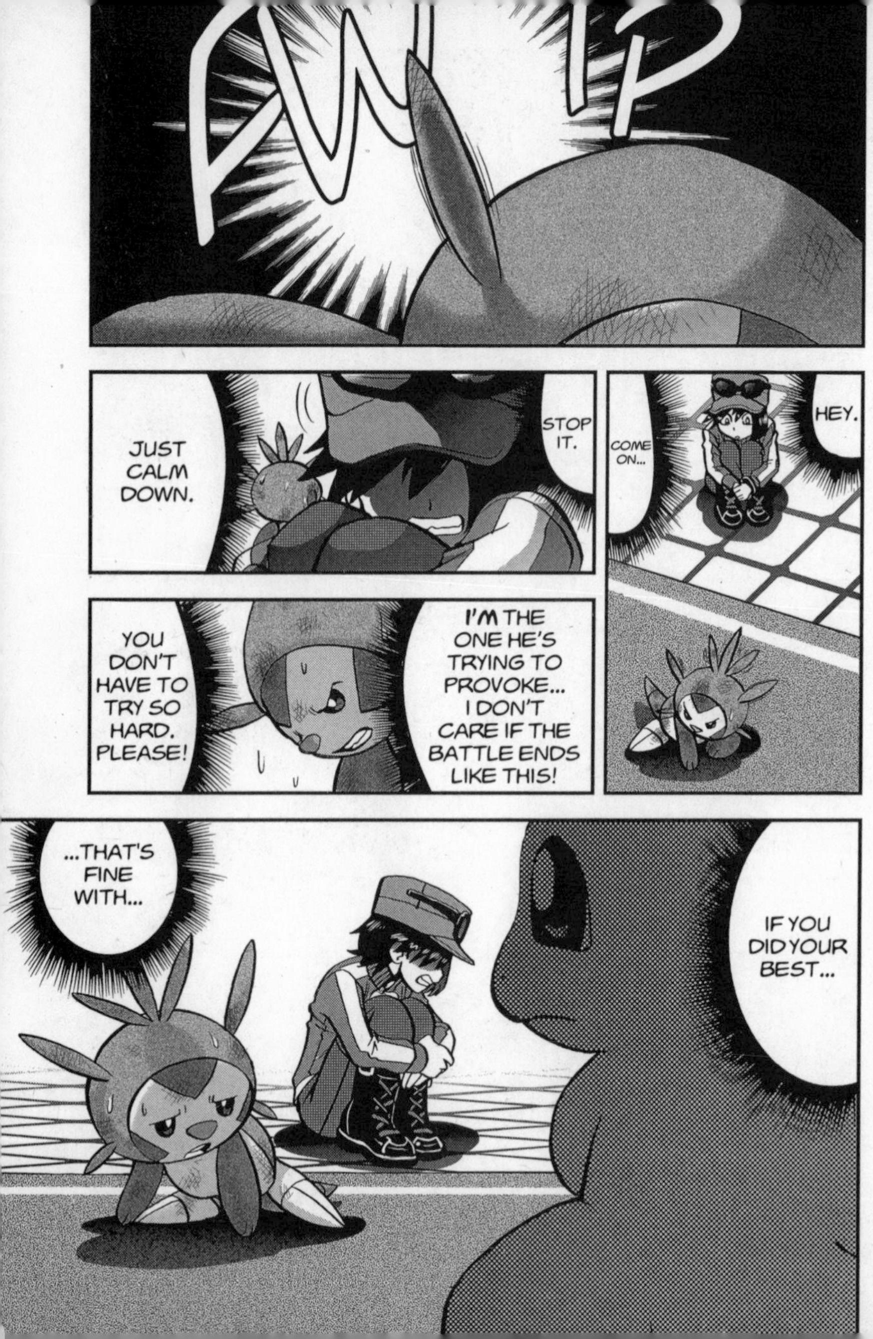
HEY.
COME ON...
STOP IT.
JUST CALM DOWN.
I'M THE ONE HE'S TRYING TO PROVOKE... I DON'T CARE IF THE BATTLE ENDS LIKE THIS!
YOU DON'T HAVE TO TRY SO HARD. PLEASE!
IF YOU DID YOUR BEST...
...THAT'S FINE WITH...

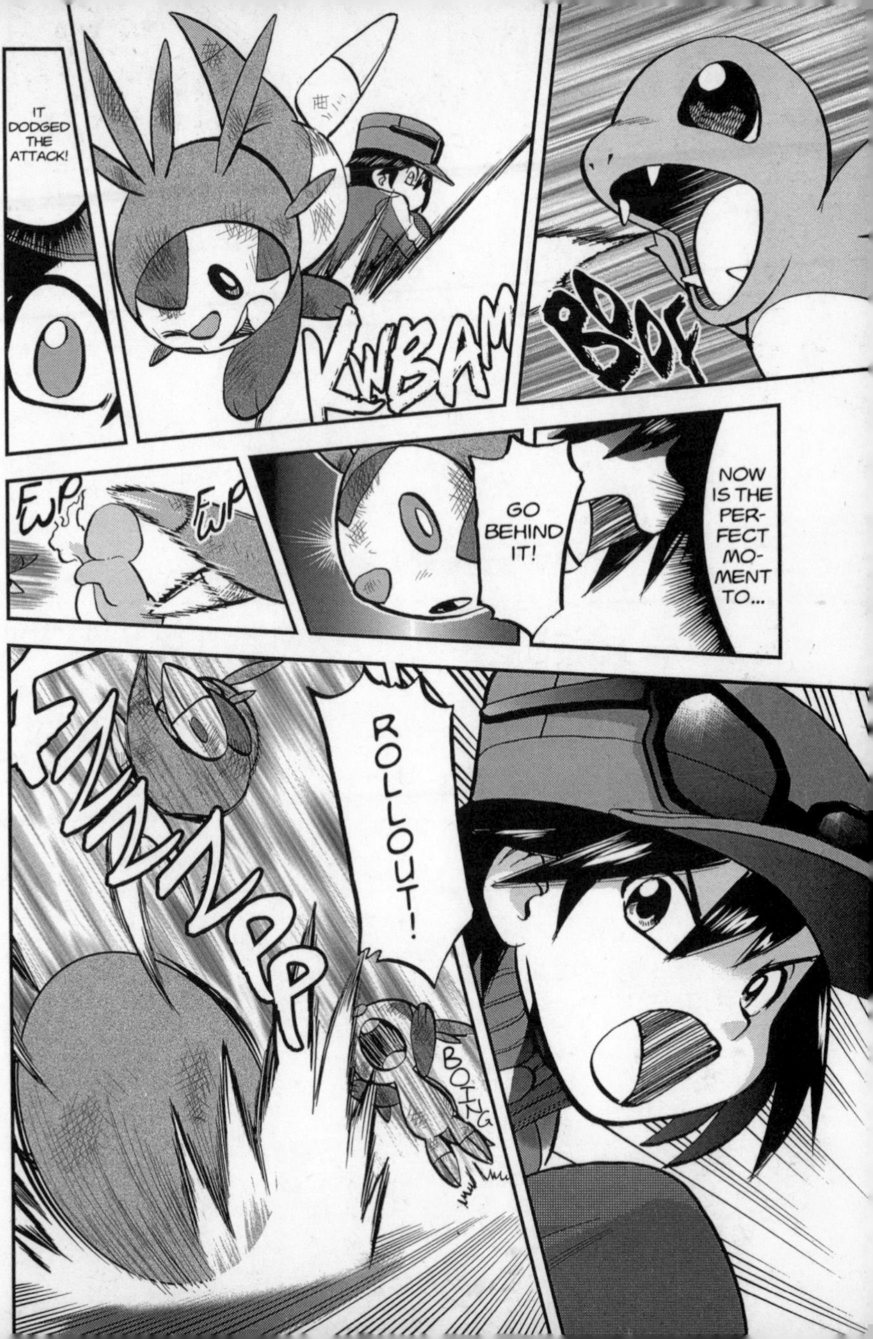
BOF
KWBAM
IT DODGED THE ATTACK!
NOW IS THE PER-FECT MO-MENT TO...
GO BEHIND IT!
FWP
FWP
ROLLOUT!
BOING

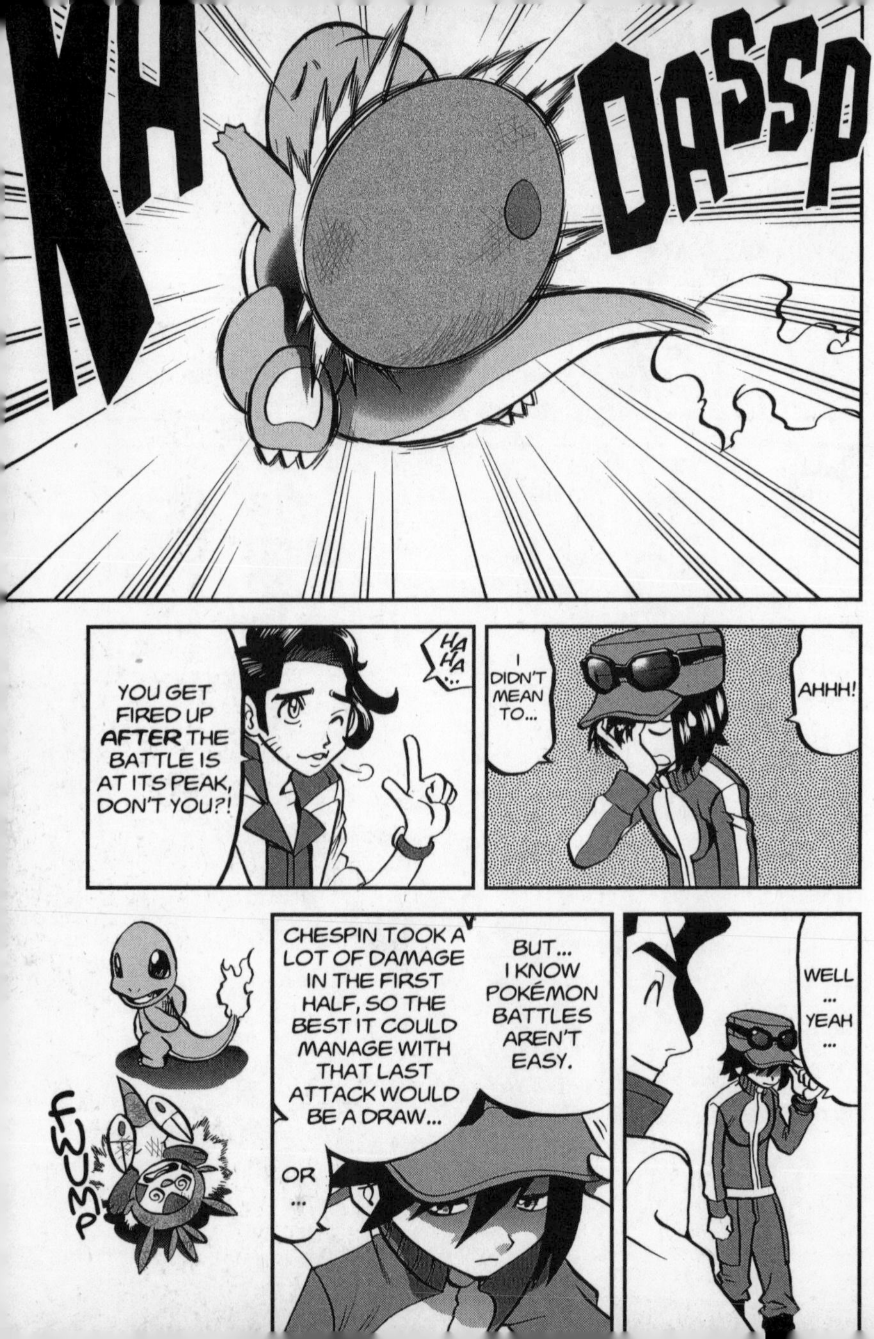
KA DASSP
AHHH!
I DIDN'T MEAN TO...
HA HA...
YOU GET FIRED UP **AFTER** THE BATTLE IS AT ITS PEAK, DON'T YOU?!
WELL ... YEAH ...
BUT... I KNOW POKÉMON BATTLES AREN'T EASY.
CHESPIN TOOK A LOT OF DAMAGE IN THE FIRST HALF, SO THE BEST IT COULD MANAGE WITH THAT LAST ATTACK WOULD BE A DRAW...
OR ...
FWUMP

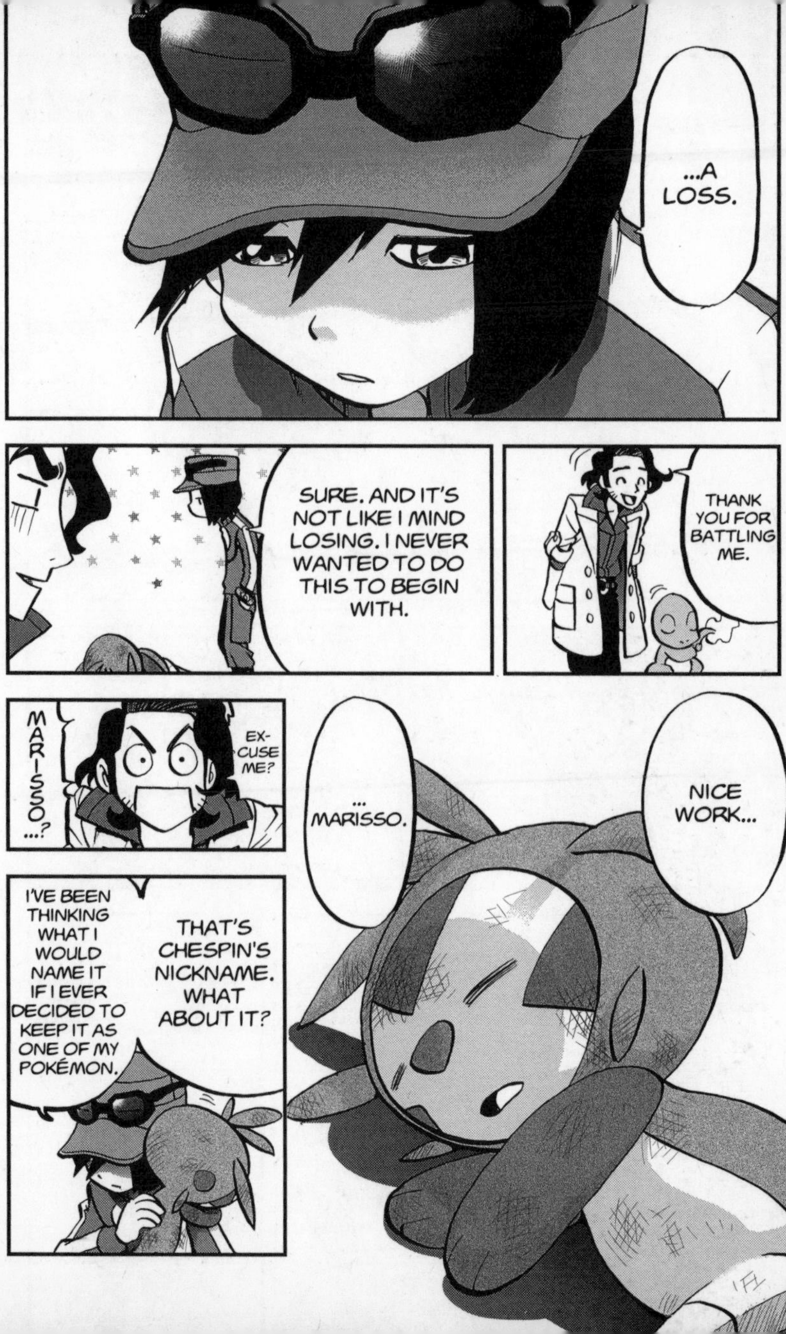
...A LOSS.
THANK YOU FOR BATTLING ME.
SURE. AND IT'S NOT LIKE I MIND LOSING. I NEVER WANTED TO DO THIS TO BEGIN WITH.
NICE WORK...
... MARISSO.
EX-CUSE ME?
MARISSO...?
THAT'S CHESPIN'S NICKNAME. WHAT ABOUT IT?
I'VE BEEN THINKING WHAT I WOULD NAME IT IF I EVER DECIDED TO KEEP IT AS ONE OF MY POKÉMON.

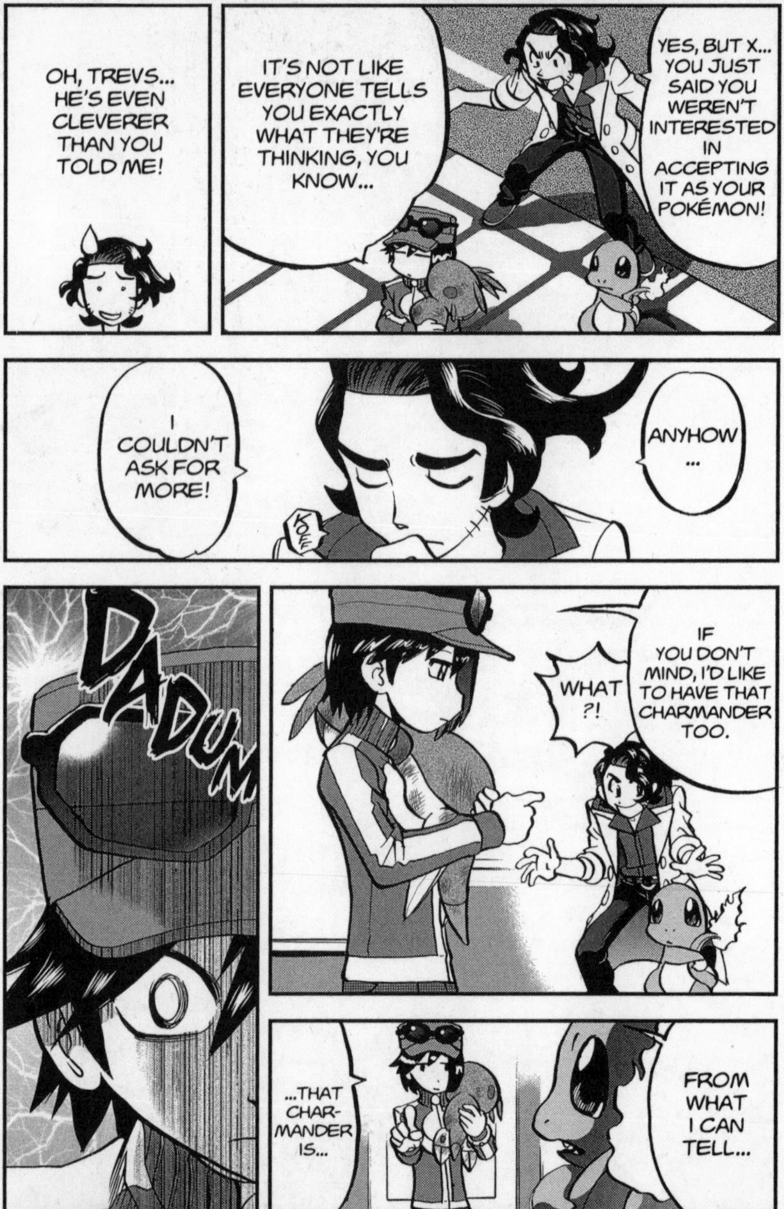
YES, BUT X... YOU JUST SAID YOU WEREN'T INTERESTED IN ACCEPTING IT AS YOUR POKÉMON!
IT'S NOT LIKE EVERYONE TELLS YOU EXACTLY WHAT THEY'RE THINKING, YOU KNOW...
OH, TREVS... HE'S EVEN CLEVERER THAN YOU TOLD ME!
ANYHOW ...
I COULDN'T ASK FOR MORE!
KOFF
IF YOU DON'T MIND, I'D LIKE TO HAVE THAT CHARMANDER TOO.
WHAT ?!
FROM WHAT I CAN TELL...
...THAT CHAR-MANDER IS...
DADUM

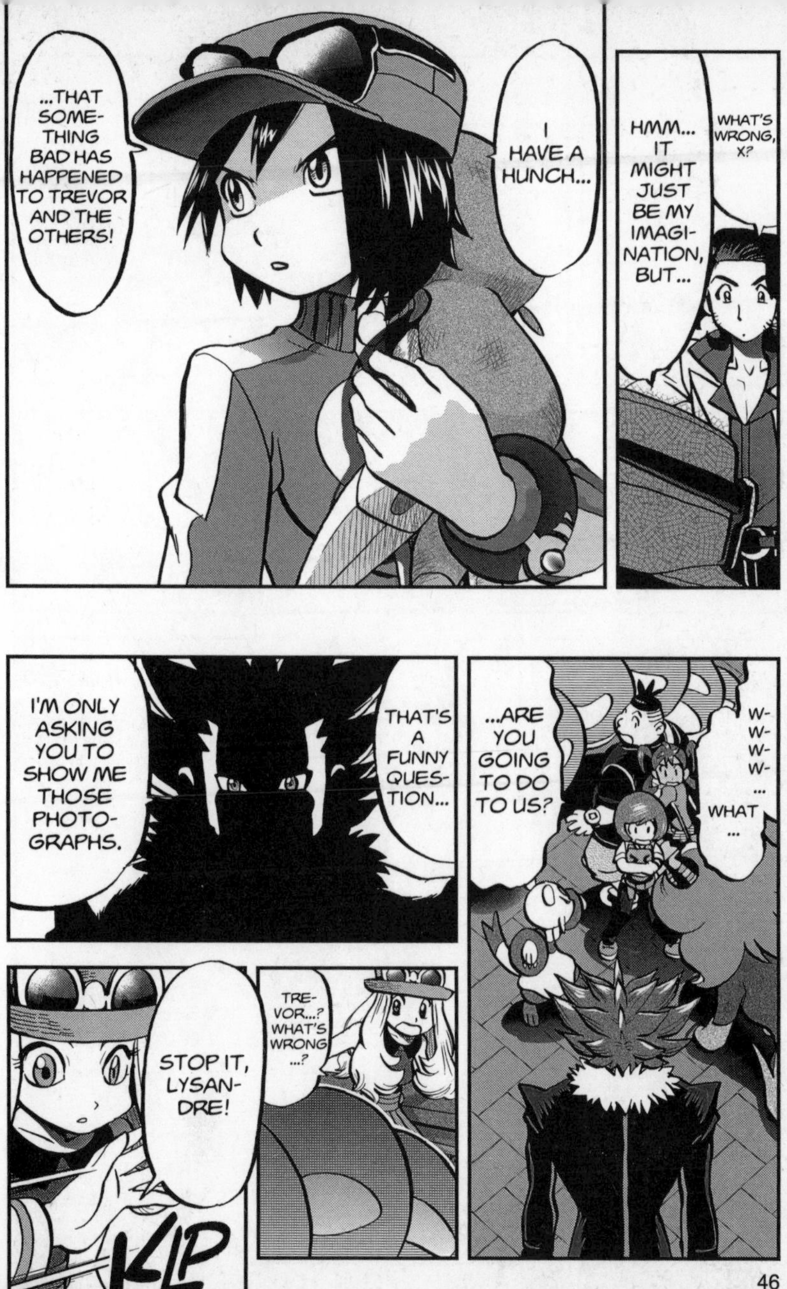
WHAT'S WRONG, X?
HMM... IT MIGHT JUST BE MY IMAGINATION, BUT...
I HAVE A HUNCH...
...THAT SOMETHING BAD HAS HAPPENED TO TREVOR AND THE OTHERS!
W-W-W-W-... WHAT ...
...ARE YOU GOING TO DO TO US?
THAT'S A FUNNY QUESTION...
I'M ONLY ASKING YOU TO SHOW ME THOSE PHOTOGRAPHS.
TREVOR...? WHAT'S WRONG ...?
STOP IT, LYSANDRE!
KLP

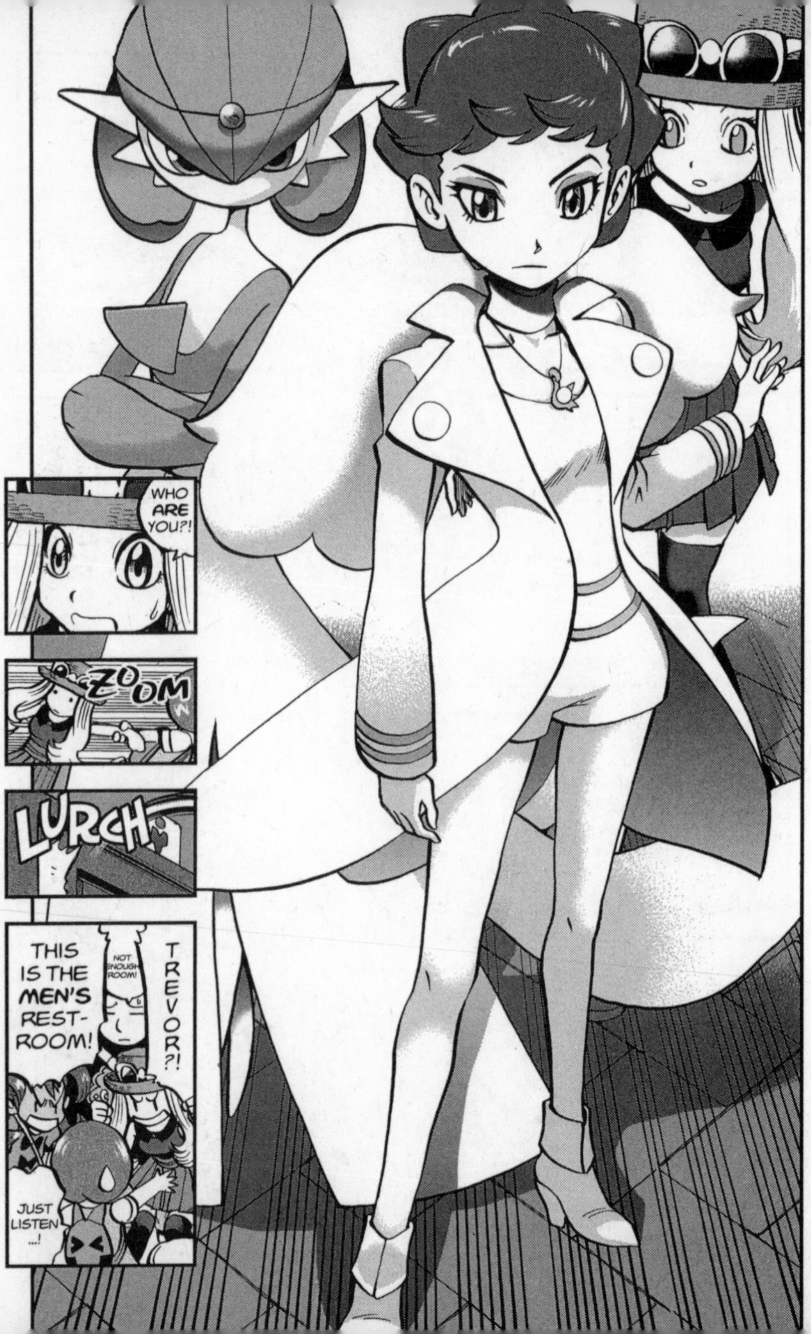
WHO ARE YOU?!
ZOOM
LURCH
TREVOR?!
NOT ENOUGH ROOM!
THIS IS THE MEN'S REST-ROOM!
JUST LISTEN...!

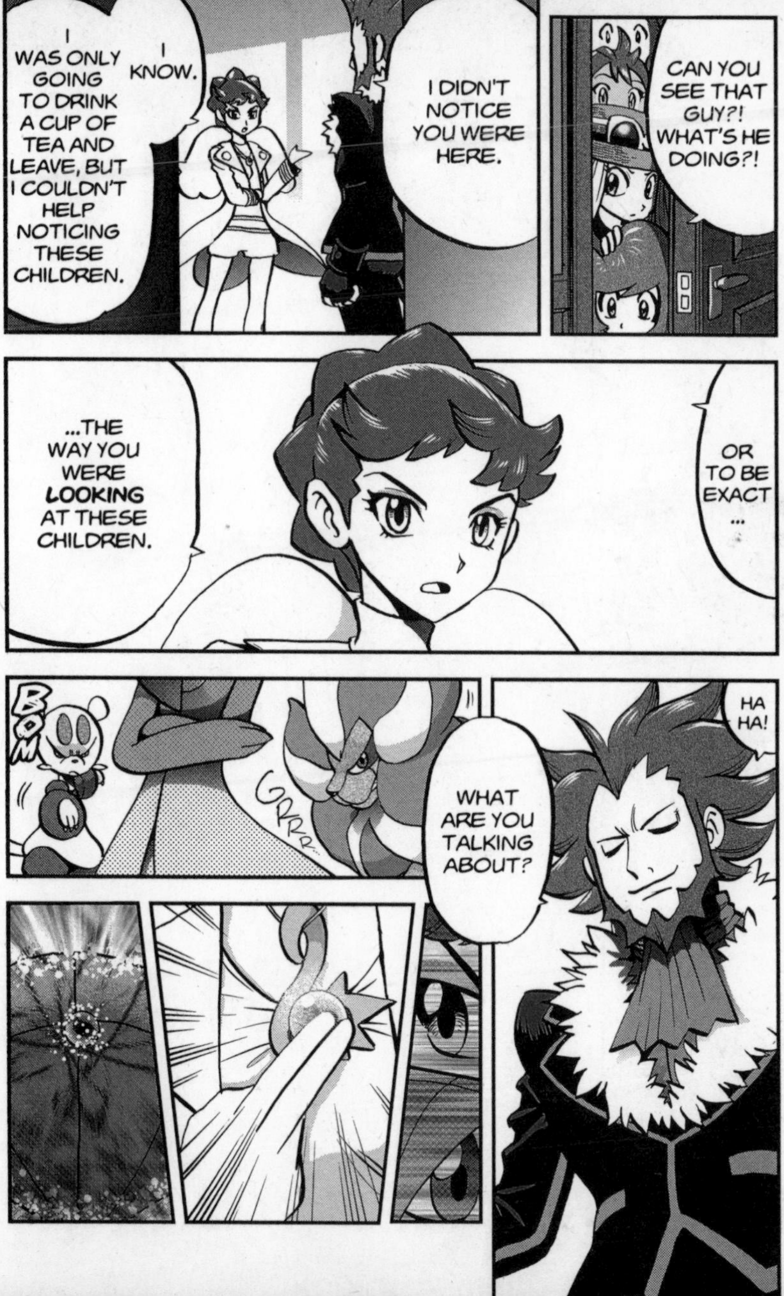
CAN YOU SEE THAT GUY?! WHAT'S HE DOING?!
I DIDN'T NOTICE YOU WERE HERE.
I KNOW.
I WAS ONLY GOING TO DRINK A CUP OF TEA AND LEAVE, BUT I COULDN'T HELP NOTICING THESE CHILDREN.
OR TO BE EXACT...
...THE WAY YOU WERE **LOOKING** AT THESE CHILDREN.
HA HA!
WHAT ARE YOU TALKING ABOUT?
BOOM
GRRRR...

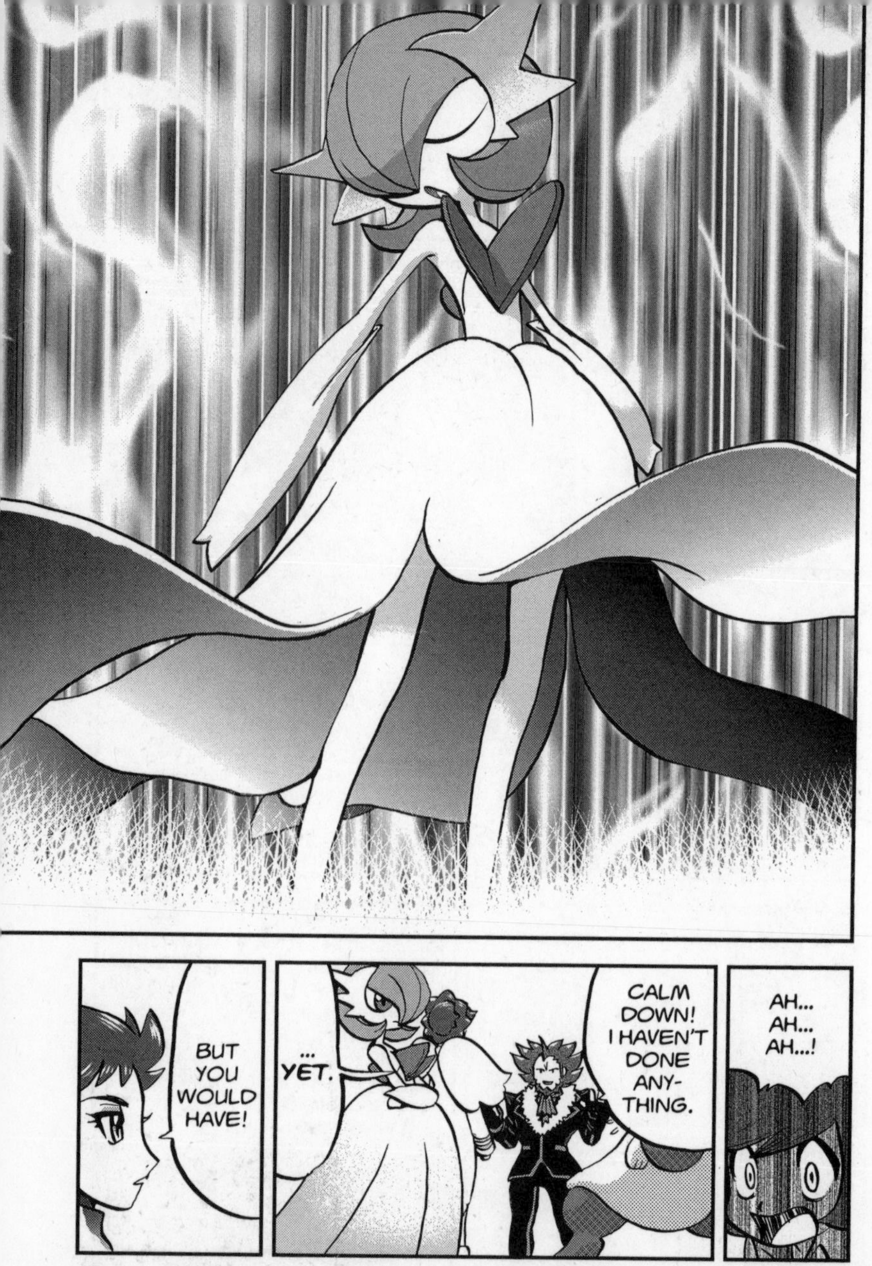
AH... AH... AH...!
CALM DOWN! I HAVEN'T DONE ANY-THING.
... YET.
BUT YOU WOULD HAVE!

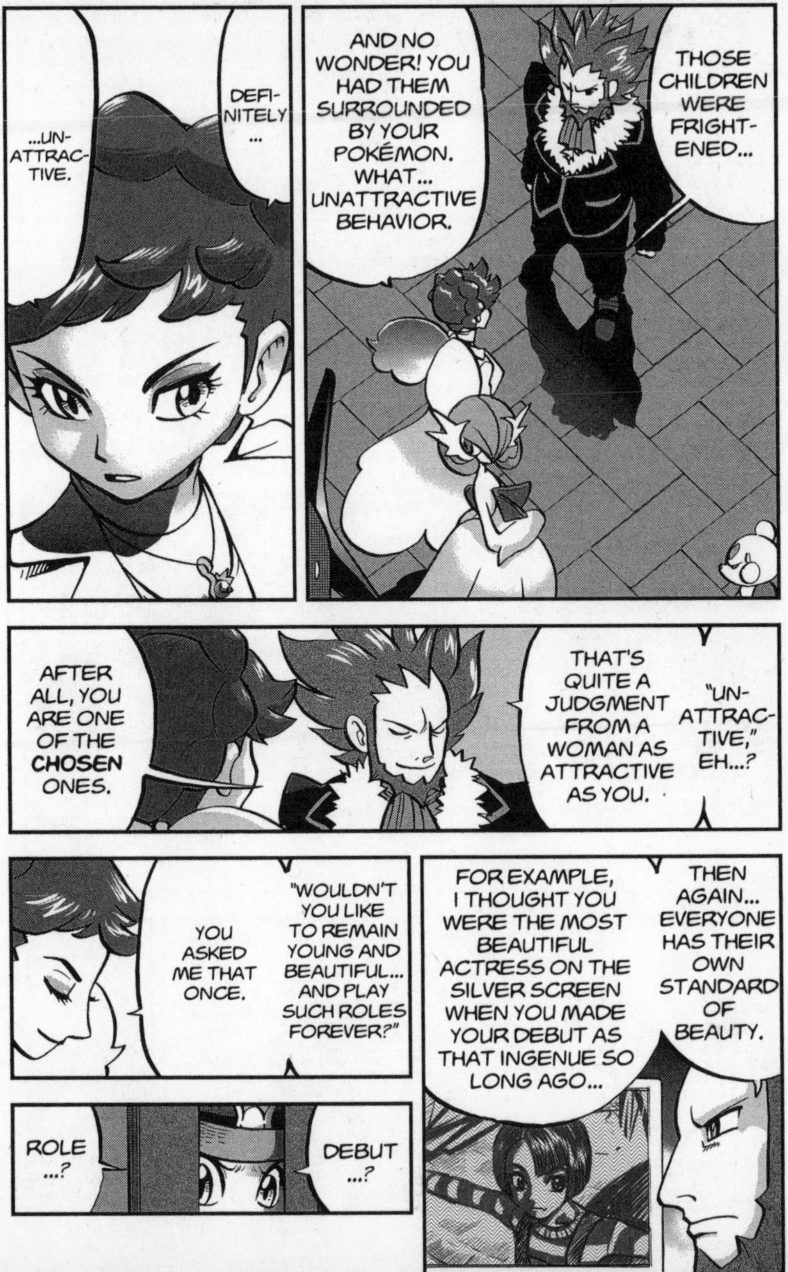
THOSE CHILDREN WERE FRIGHTENED...
AND NO WONDER! YOU HAD THEM SURROUNDED BY YOUR POKÉMON. WHAT... UNATTRACTIVE BEHAVIOR.
DEFINITELY...
...UNATTRACTIVE.
"UNATTRACTIVE," EH...?
THAT'S QUITE A JUDGMENT FROM A WOMAN AS ATTRACTIVE AS YOU.
AFTER ALL, YOU ARE ONE OF THE **CHOSEN** ONES.
THEN AGAIN... EVERYONE HAS THEIR OWN STANDARD OF BEAUTY.
FOR EXAMPLE, I THOUGHT YOU WERE THE MOST BEAUTIFUL ACTRESS ON THE SILVER SCREEN WHEN YOU MADE YOUR DEBUT AS THAT INGENUE SO LONG AGO...
"WOULDN'T YOU LIKE TO REMAIN YOUNG AND BEAUTIFUL... AND PLAY SUCH ROLES FOREVER?"
YOU ASKED ME THAT ONCE.
DEBUT ...?
ROLE ...?

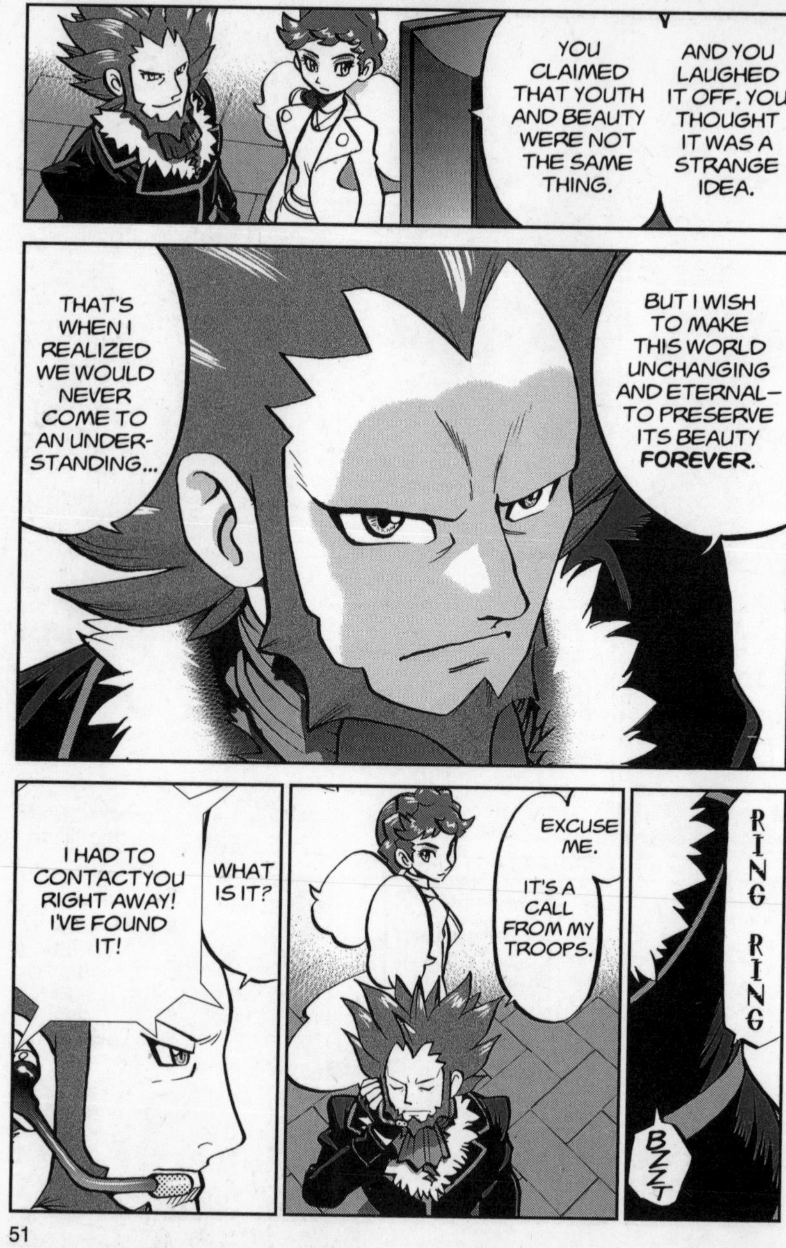
YOU CLAIMED THAT YOUTH AND BEAUTY WERE NOT THE SAME THING.
AND YOU LAUGHED IT OFF. YOU THOUGHT IT WAS A STRANGE IDEA.
THAT'S WHEN I REALIZED WE WOULD NEVER COME TO AN UNDER-STANDING...
BUT I WISH TO MAKE THIS WORLD UNCHANGING AND ETERNAL— TO PRESERVE ITS BEAUTY **FOREVER.**
RING RING RING
BZZT
EXCUSE ME.
IT'S A CALL FROM MY TROOPS.
WHAT IS IT?
I HAD TO CONTACT YOU RIGHT AWAY! I'VE FOUND IT!

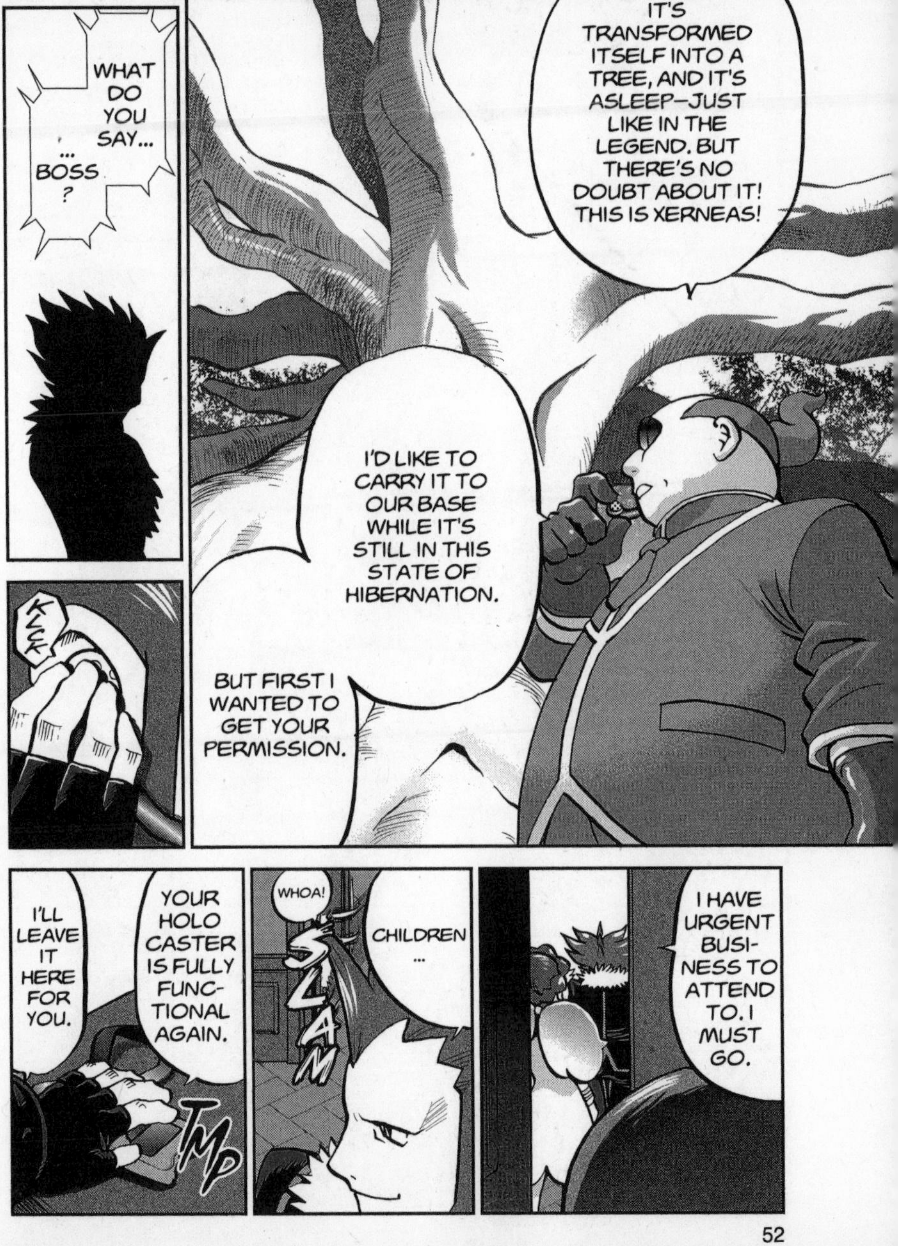
IT'S TRANSFORMED ITSELF INTO A TREE, AND IT'S ASLEEP—JUST LIKE IN THE LEGEND. BUT THERE'S NO DOUBT ABOUT IT! THIS IS XERNEAS!
I'D LIKE TO CARRY IT TO OUR BASE WHILE IT'S STILL IN THIS STATE OF HIBERNATION.
BUT FIRST I WANTED TO GET YOUR PERMISSION.
WHAT DO YOU SAY... ...BOSS?
KLCK
I HAVE URGENT BUSINESS TO ATTEND TO. I MUST GO.
CHILDREN...
WHOA!
SLAM
YOUR HOLO CASTER IS FULLY FUNCTIONAL AGAIN.
I'LL LEAVE IT HERE FOR YOU.
TMP

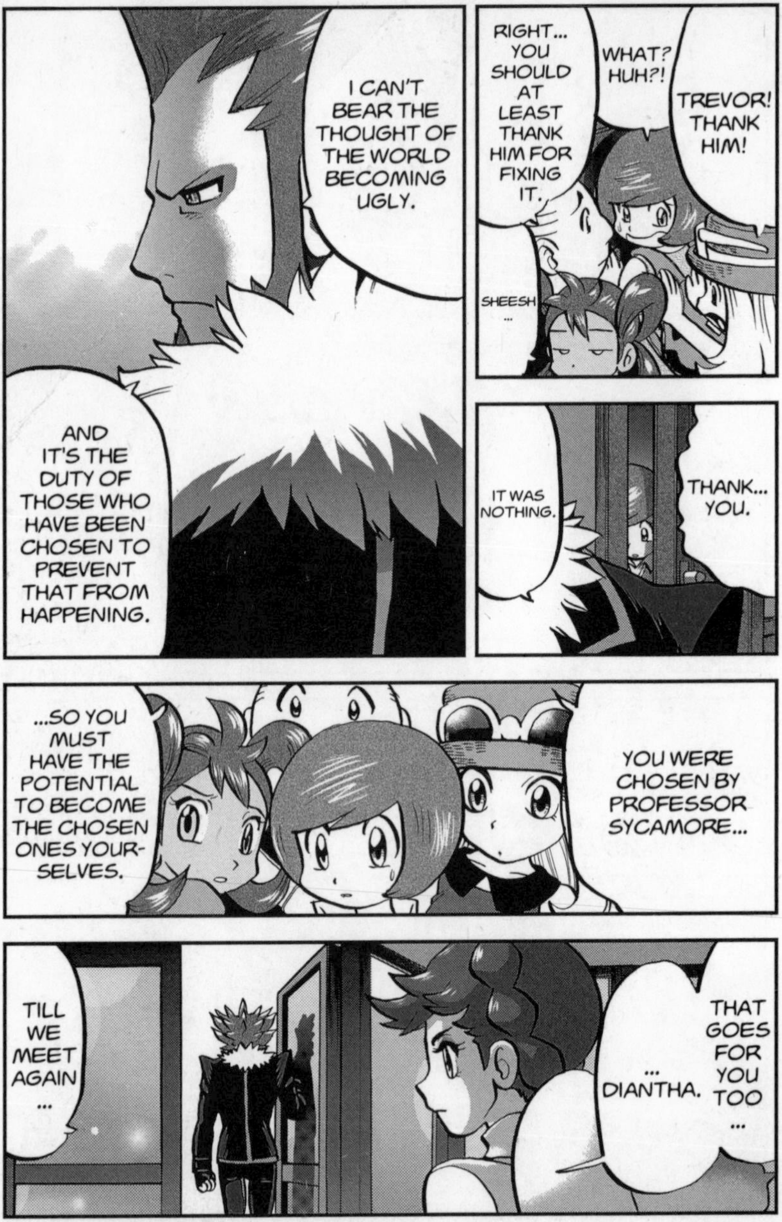
TREVOR! THANK HIM!
WHAT? HUH?!
RIGHT... YOU SHOULD AT LEAST THANK HIM FOR FIXING IT.
SHEESH...
THANK... YOU.
IT WAS NOTHING.
I CAN'T BEAR THE THOUGHT OF THE WORLD BECOMING UGLY.
AND IT'S THE DUTY OF THOSE WHO HAVE BEEN CHOSEN TO PREVENT THAT FROM HAPPENING.
YOU WERE CHOSEN BY PROFESSOR SYCAMORE...
...SO YOU MUST HAVE THE POTENTIAL TO BECOME THE CHOSEN ONES YOURSELVES.
THAT GOES FOR YOU TOO...
...DIANTHA.
TILL WE MEET AGAIN...

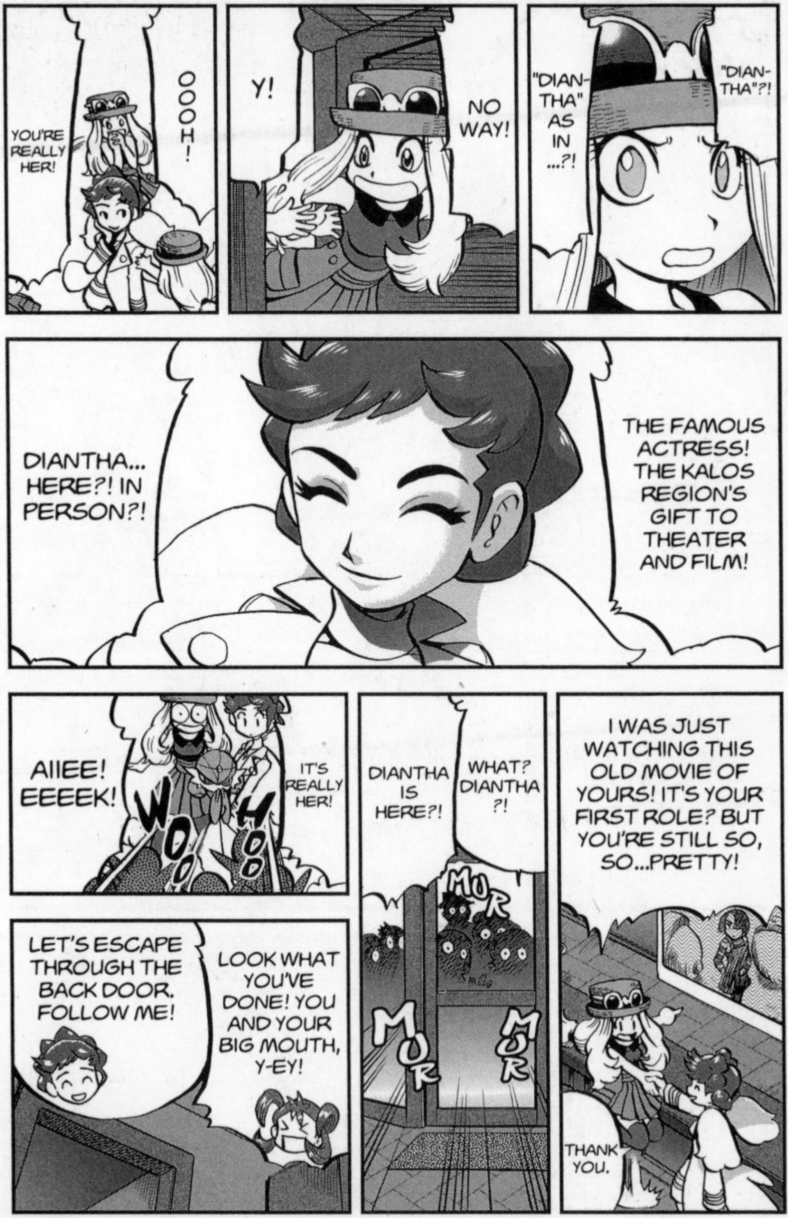
"DIAN-THA"?!
"DIAN-THA" AS IN ...?!
NO WAY!
Y!
OOOH!
YOU'RE REALLY HER!
THE FAMOUS ACTRESS! THE KALOS REGION'S GIFT TO THEATER AND FILM!
DIANTHA... HERE?! IN PERSON?!
I WAS JUST WATCHING THIS OLD MOVIE OF YOURS! IT'S YOUR FIRST ROLE? BUT YOU'RE STILL SO, SO...PRETTY!
THANK YOU.
WHAT? DIANTHA?!
DIANTHA IS HERE?!
MUR
MUR
MUR
IT'S REALLY HER!
AIIEE! EEEEK!
WOO
HOO
LOOK WHAT YOU'VE DONE! YOU AND YOUR BIG MOUTH, Y-EY!
LET'S ESCAPE THROUGH THE BACK DOOR. FOLLOW ME!

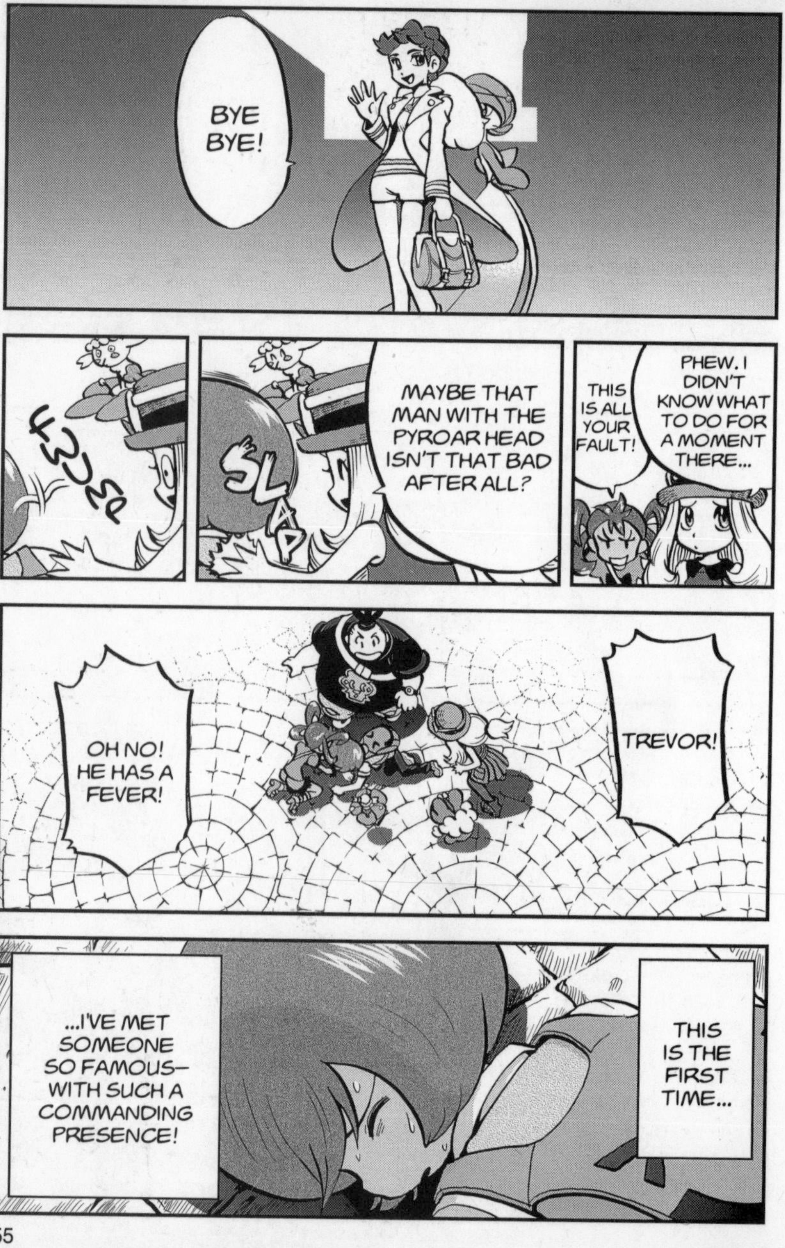
BYE BYE!
PHEW. I DIDN'T KNOW WHAT TO DO FOR A MOMENT THERE...
THIS IS ALL YOUR FAULT!
MAYBE THAT MAN WITH THE PYROAR HEAD ISN'T THAT BAD AFTER ALL?
SLAP
FWUMP
TREVOR!
OH NO! HE HAS A FEVER!
THIS IS THE FIRST TIME...
...I'VE MET SOMEONE SO FAMOUS—WITH SUCH A COMMANDING PRESENCE!

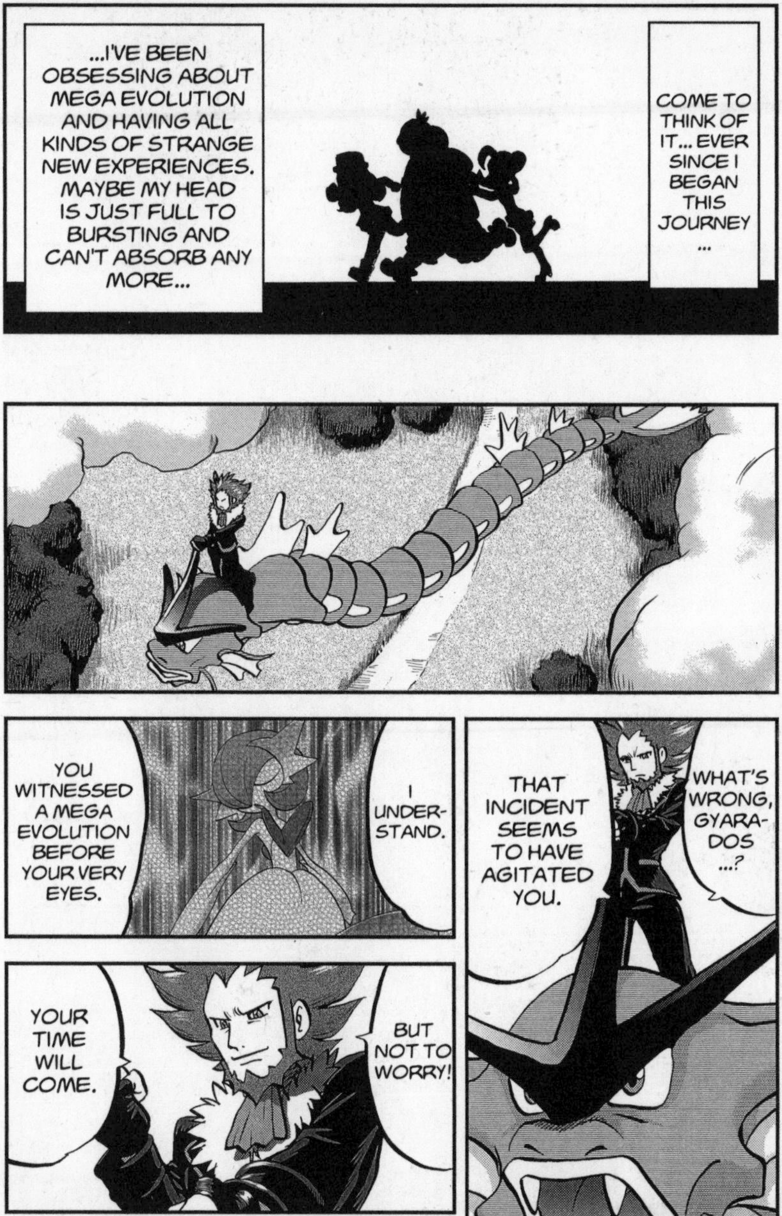
COME TO THINK OF IT... EVER SINCE I BEGAN THIS JOURNEY ...
...I'VE BEEN OBSESSING ABOUT MEGA EVOLUTION AND HAVING ALL KINDS OF STRANGE NEW EXPERIENCES. MAYBE MY HEAD IS JUST FULL TO BURSTING AND CAN'T ABSORB ANY MORE...
WHAT'S WRONG, GYARADOS ...?
THAT INCIDENT SEEMS TO HAVE AGITATED YOU.
I UNDERSTAND.
YOU WITNESSED A MEGA EVOLUTION BEFORE YOUR VERY EYES.
BUT NOT TO WORRY!
YOUR TIME WILL COME.

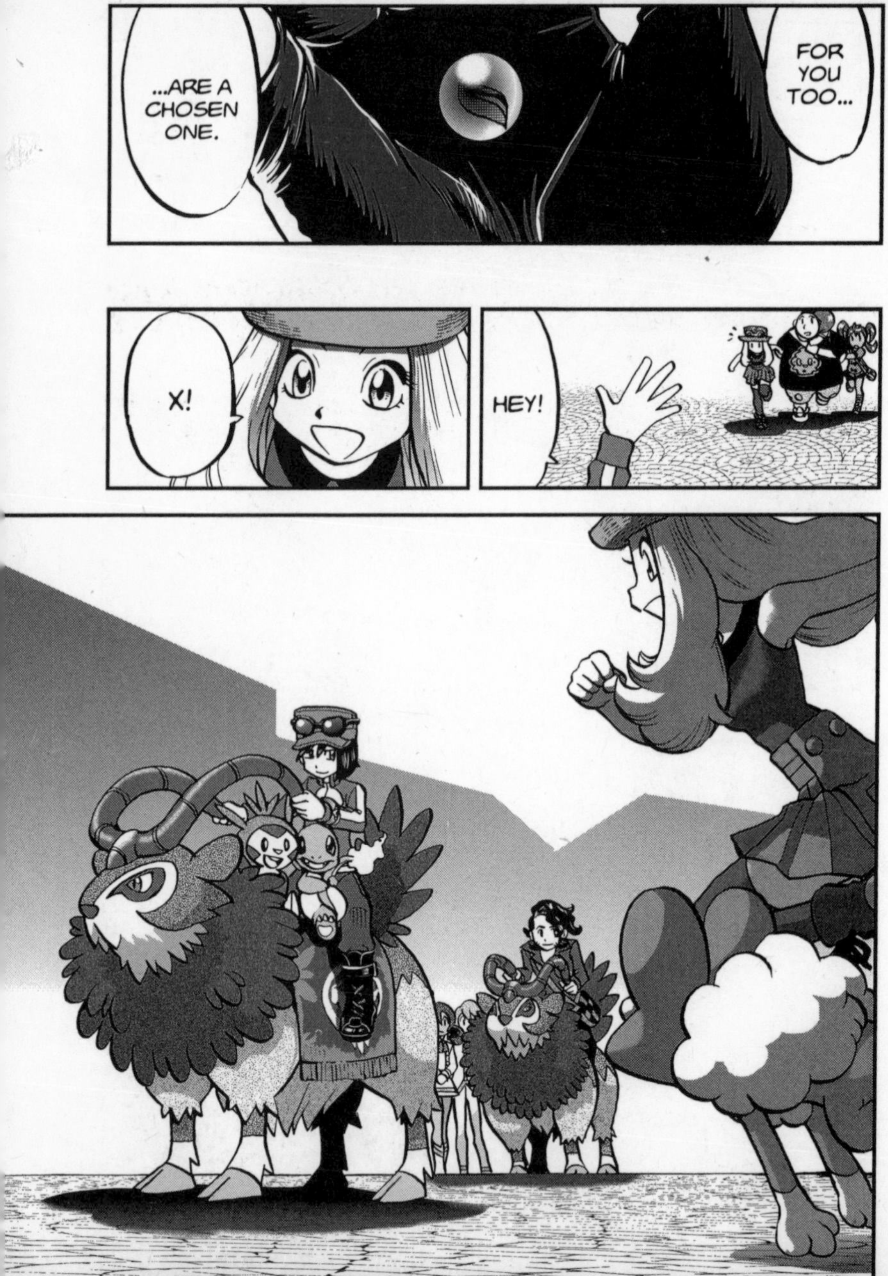
FOR YOU TOO...
...ARE A CHOSEN ONE.
HEY!
X!

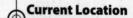

## Current Location

**Lumiose City**

A dazzling metropolis of art and artifice, located in the very heart of the Kalos region.

# Adventure 10 Pangoro Poses a Problem

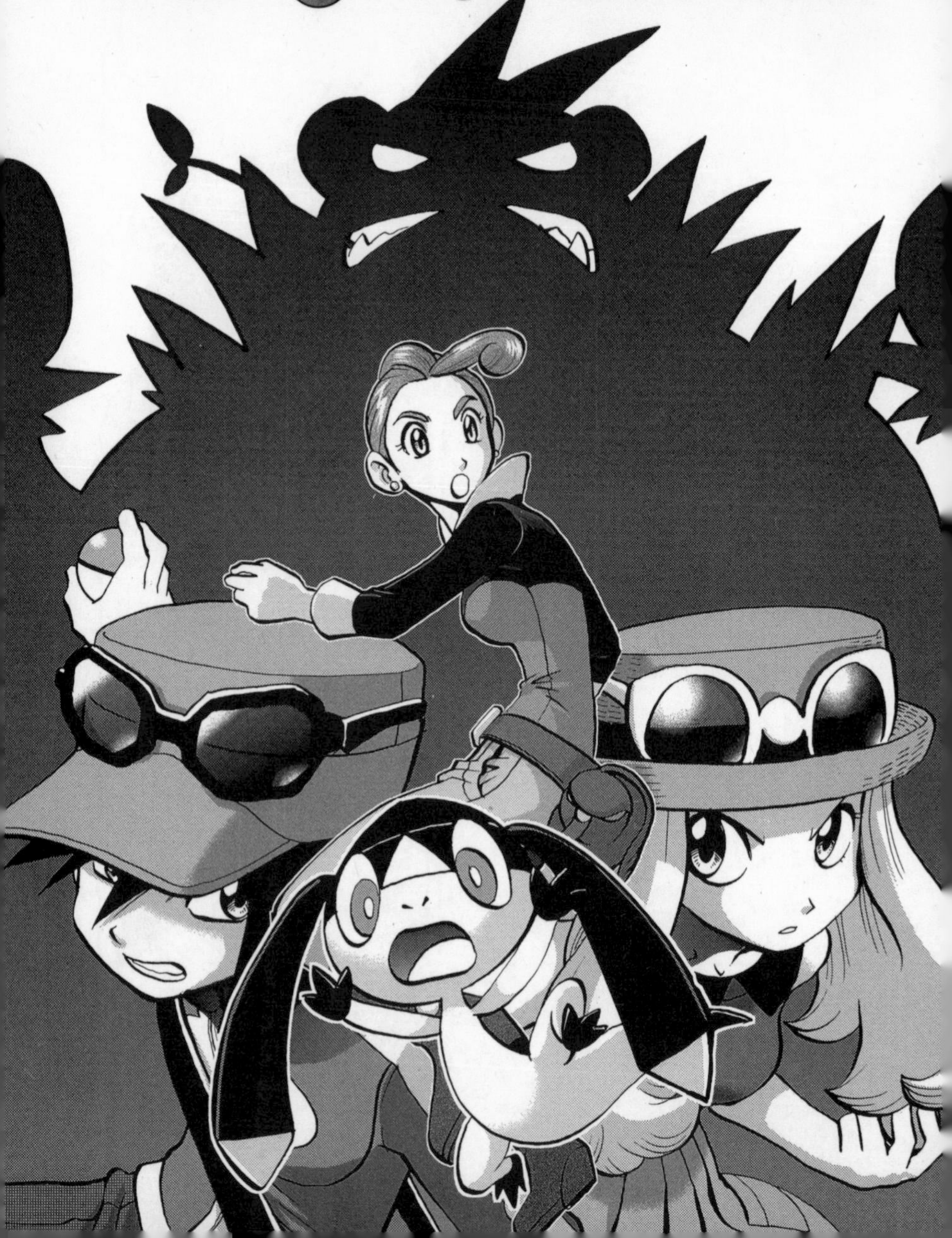

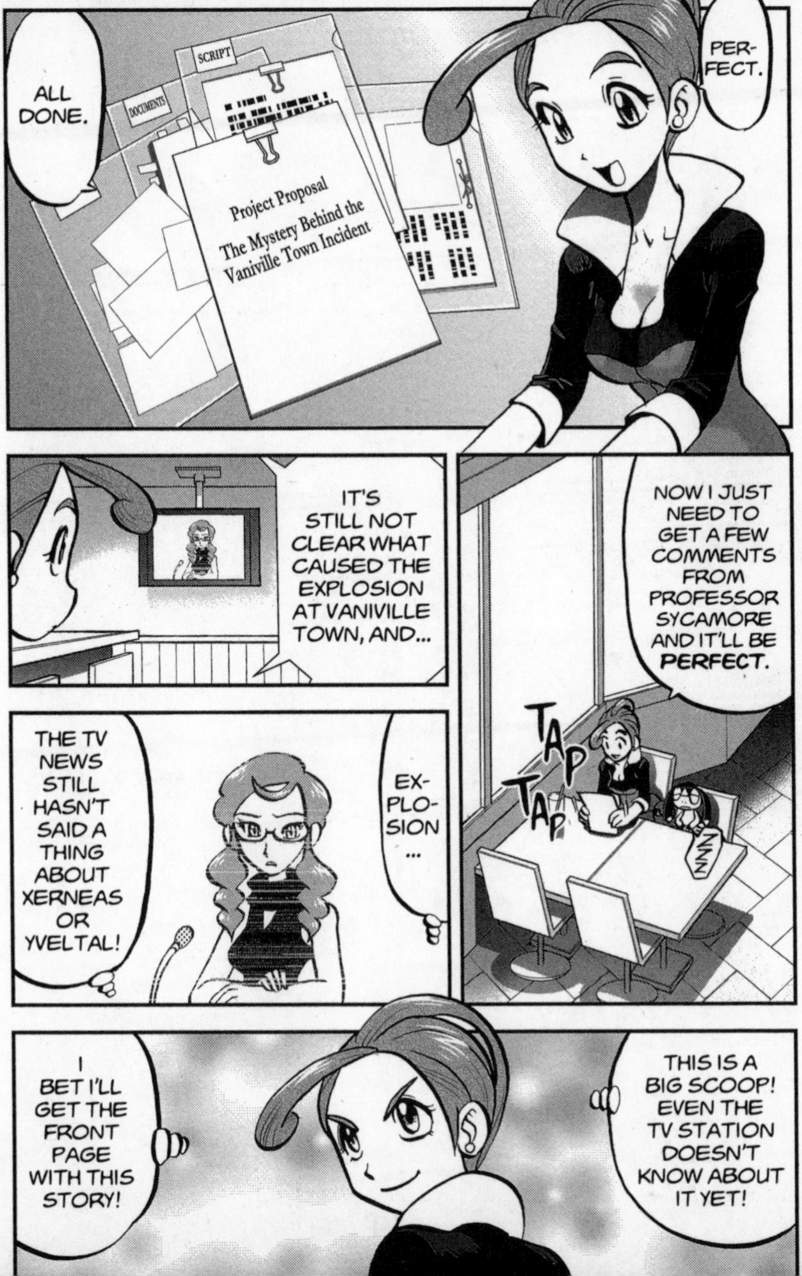
PER-
FECT.
ALL DONE.
SCRIPT
DOCUMENTS
Project Proposal
The Mystery Behind the Vaniville Town Incident
NOW I JUST NEED TO GET A FEW COMMENTS FROM PROFESSOR SYCAMORE AND IT'LL BE **PERFECT.**
TAP TAP
ZZZ
IT'S STILL NOT CLEAR WHAT CAUSED THE EXPLOSION AT VANIVILLE TOWN, AND...
EX-PLO-SION...
THE TV NEWS STILL HASN'T SAID A THING ABOUT XERNEAS OR YVELTAL!
THIS IS A BIG SCOOP! EVEN THE TV STATION DOESN'T KNOW ABOUT IT YET!
I BET I'LL GET THE FRONT PAGE WITH THIS STORY!

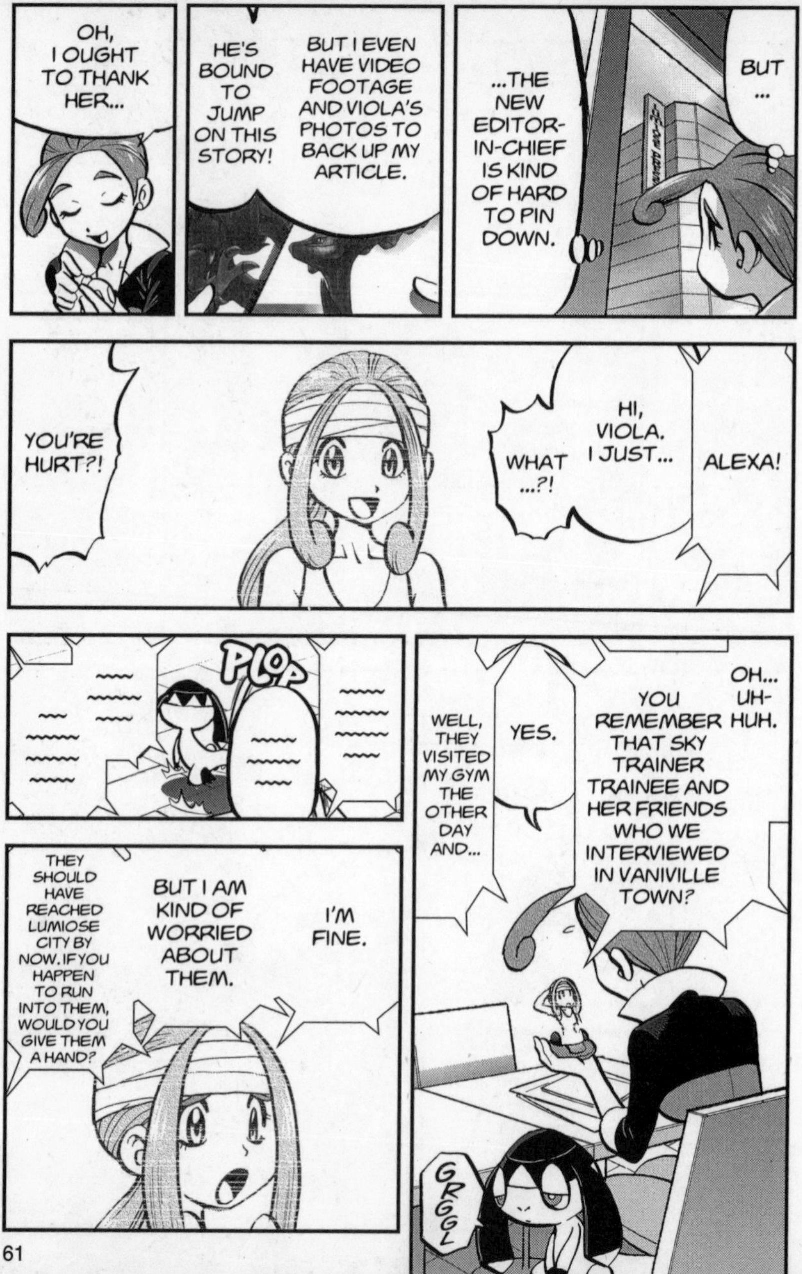
BUT ...
...THE NEW EDITOR-IN-CHIEF IS KIND OF HARD TO PIN DOWN.
BUT I EVEN HAVE VIDEO FOOTAGE AND VIOLA'S PHOTOS TO BACK UP MY ARTICLE.
HE'S BOUND TO JUMP ON THIS STORY!
OH, I OUGHT TO THANK HER...
ALEXA!
HI, VIOLA. I JUST...
WHAT ...?!
YOU'RE HURT?!
OH... UH-HUH.
YOU REMEMBER THAT SKY TRAINER TRAINEE AND HER FRIENDS WHO WE INTERVIEWED IN VANIVILLE TOWN?
YES.
WELL, THEY VISITED MY GYM THE OTHER DAY AND...
GRGGL
PLOP
I'M FINE.
BUT I AM KIND OF WORRIED ABOUT THEM.
THEY SHOULD HAVE REACHED LUMIOSE CITY BY NOW. IF YOU HAPPEN TO RUN INTO THEM, WOULD YOU GIVE THEM A HAND?

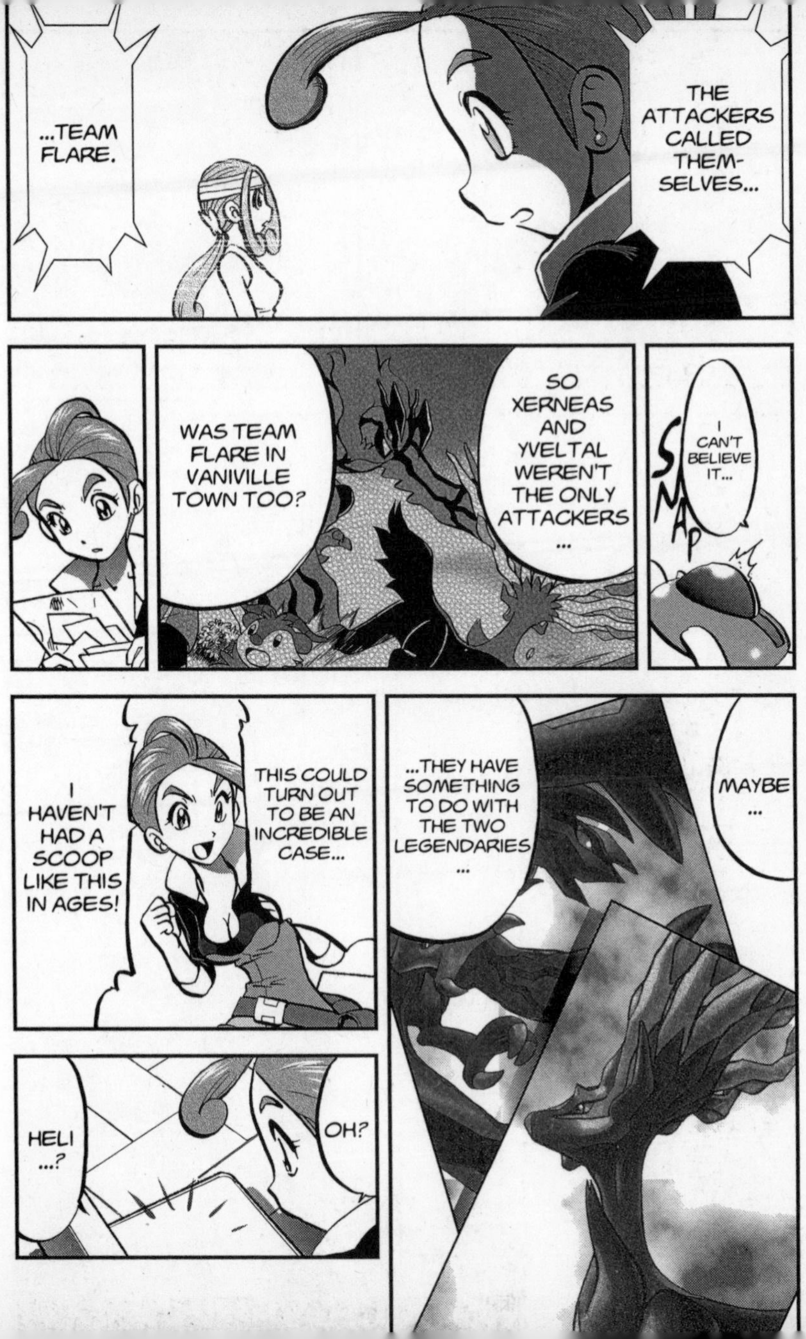
THE ATTACKERS CALLED THEM-SELVES...
...TEAM FLARE.
I CAN'T BELIEVE IT...
SNAP
SO XERNEAS AND YVELTAL WEREN'T THE ONLY ATTACKERS...
WAS TEAM FLARE IN VANIVILLE TOWN TOO?
MAYBE...
...THEY HAVE SOMETHING TO DO WITH THE TWO LEGENDARIES...
THIS COULD TURN OUT TO BE AN INCREDIBLE CASE...
I HAVEN'T HAD A SCOOP LIKE THIS IN AGES!
OH?
HELI...?

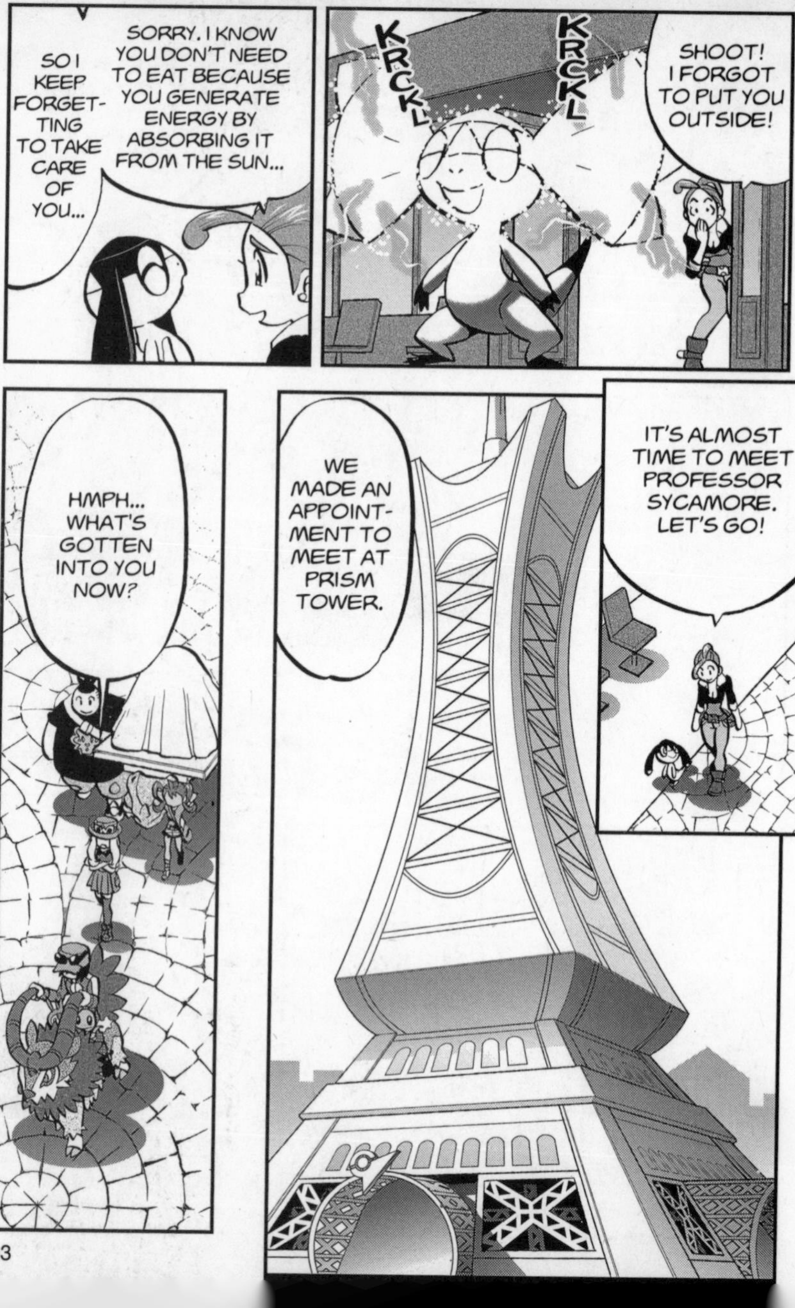
KRCKL
KRCKL
SHOOT! I FORGOT TO PUT YOU OUTSIDE!
SORRY. I KNOW YOU DON'T NEED TO EAT BECAUSE YOU GENERATE ENERGY BY ABSORBING IT FROM THE SUN...
SO I KEEP FORGETTING TO TAKE CARE OF YOU...
IT'S ALMOST TIME TO MEET PROFESSOR SYCAMORE. LET'S GO!
WE MADE AN APPOINTMENT TO MEET AT PRISM TOWER.
HMPH... WHAT'S GOTTEN INTO YOU NOW?

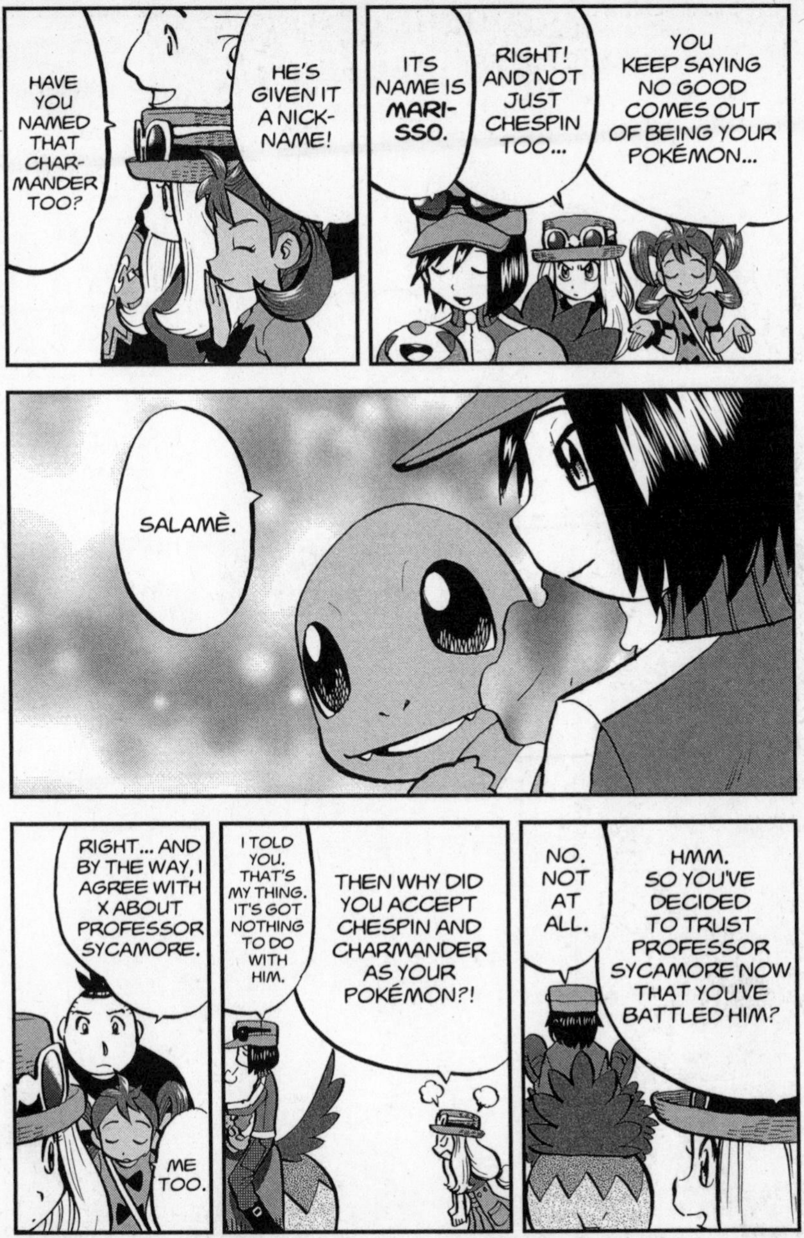
YOU KEEP SAYING NO GOOD COMES OUT OF BEING YOUR POKÉMON...
RIGHT! AND NOT JUST CHESPIN TOO...
ITS NAME IS MARI-SSO.
HE'S GIVEN IT A NICK-NAME!
HAVE YOU NAMED THAT CHAR-MANDER TOO?
SALAMÈ.
HMM. SO YOU'VE DECIDED TO TRUST PROFESSOR SYCAMORE NOW THAT YOU'VE BATTLED HIM?
NO. NOT AT ALL.
THEN WHY DID YOU ACCEPT CHESPIN AND CHARMANDER AS YOUR POKÉMON?!
I TOLD YOU. THAT'S MY THING. IT'S GOT NOTHING TO DO WITH HIM.
RIGHT... AND BY THE WAY, I AGREE WITH X ABOUT PROFESSOR SYCAMORE.
ME TOO.

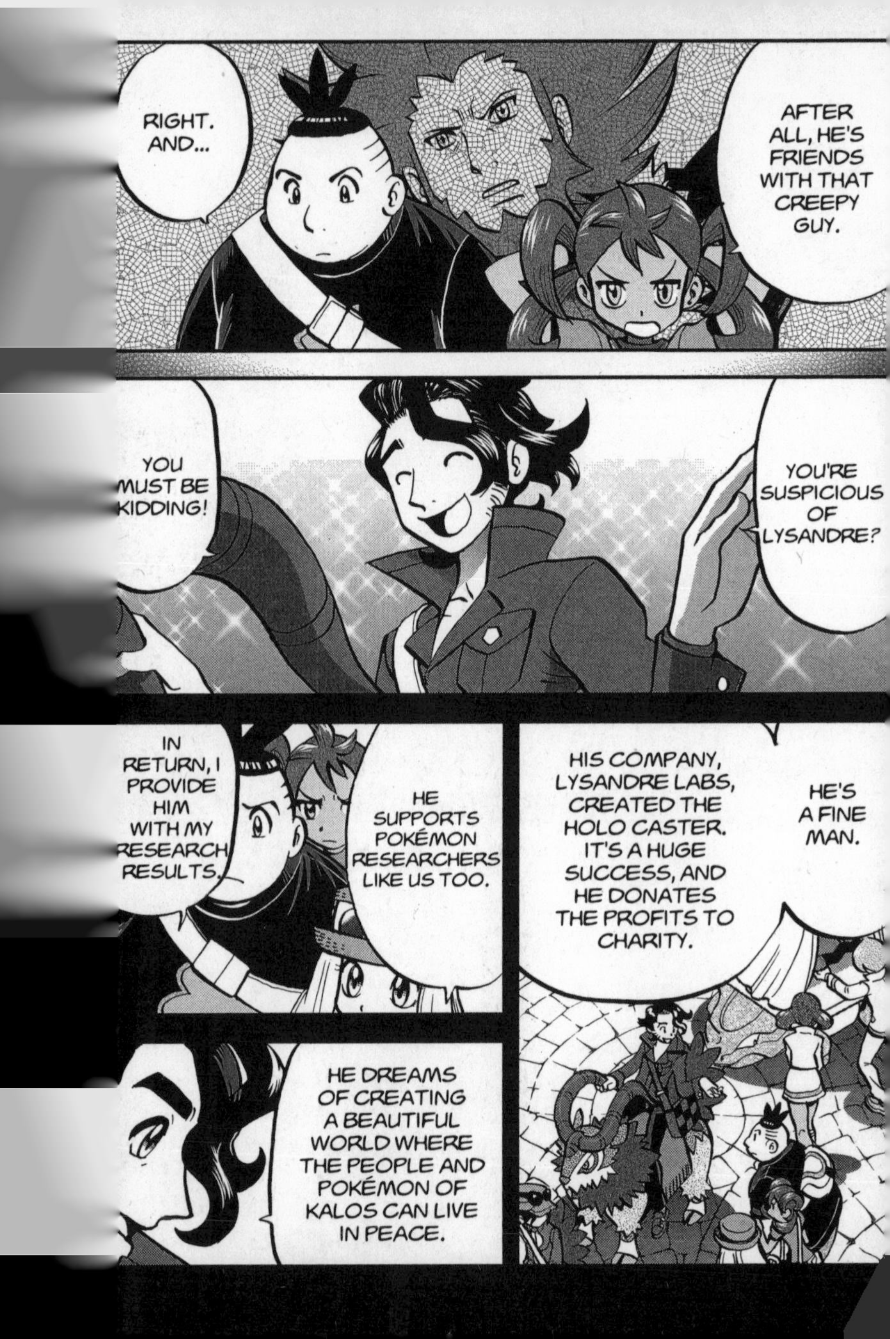
AFTER ALL, HE'S FRIENDS WITH THAT CREEPY GUY.
RIGHT. AND...
YOU'RE SUSPICIOUS OF LYSANDRE?
YOU MUST BE KIDDING!
HE'S A FINE MAN.
HIS COMPANY, LYSANDRE LABS, CREATED THE HOLO CASTER. IT'S A HUGE SUCCESS, AND HE DONATES THE PROFITS TO CHARITY.
HE SUPPORTS POKÉMON RESEARCHERS LIKE US TOO.
IN RETURN, I PROVIDE HIM WITH MY RESEARCH RESULTS.
HE DREAMS OF CREATING A BEAUTIFUL WORLD WHERE THE PEOPLE AND POKÉMON OF KALOS CAN LIVE IN PEACE.

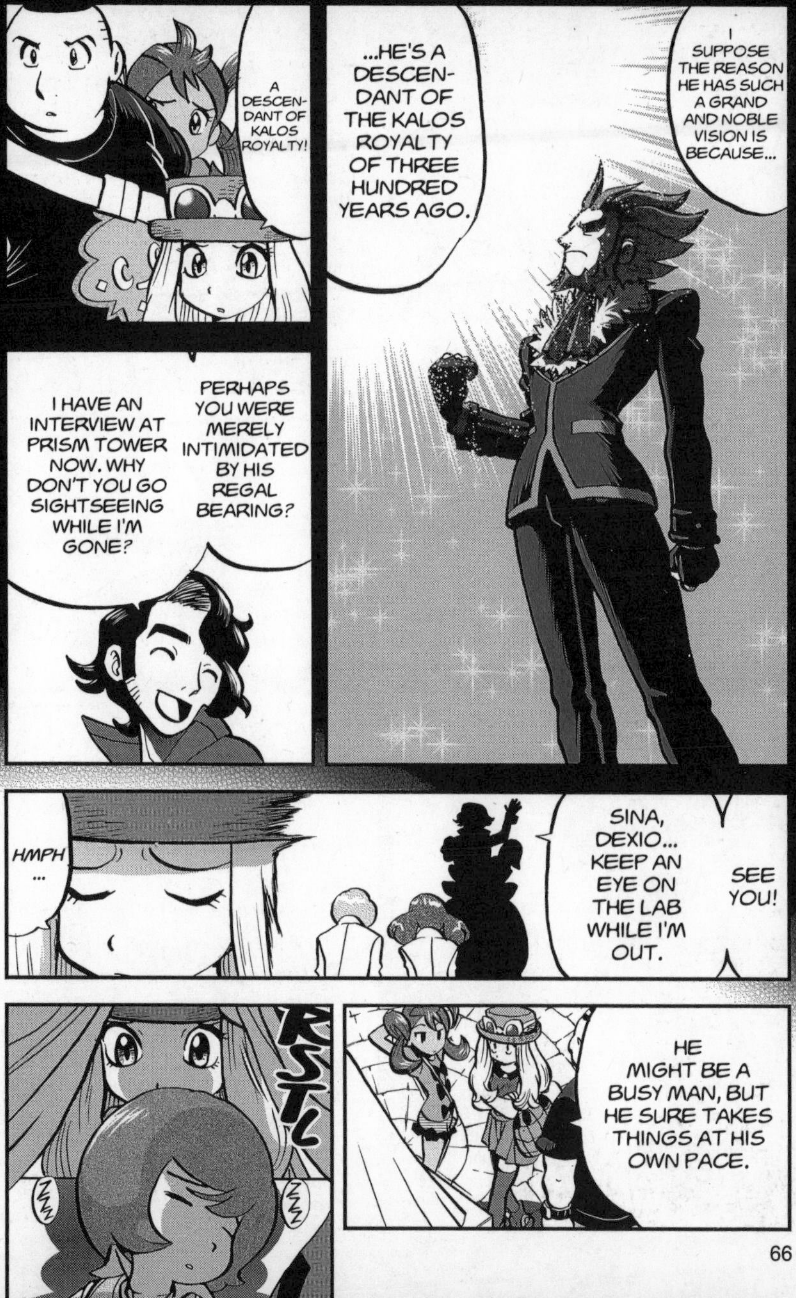
I SUPPOSE THE REASON HE HAS SUCH A GRAND AND NOBLE VISION IS BECAUSE...
...HE'S A DESCEN-DANT OF THE KALOS ROYALTY OF THREE HUNDRED YEARS AGO.
A DESCEN-DANT OF KALOS ROYALTY!
PERHAPS YOU WERE MERELY INTIMIDATED BY HIS REGAL BEARING?
I HAVE AN INTERVIEW AT PRISM TOWER NOW. WHY DON'T YOU GO SIGHTSEEING WHILE I'M GONE?
SINA, DEXIO... KEEP AN EYE ON THE LAB WHILE I'M OUT.
SEE YOU!
HMPH ...
HE MIGHT BE A BUSY MAN, BUT HE SURE TAKES THINGS AT HIS OWN PACE.
RSTL
ZZZ
ZZZ

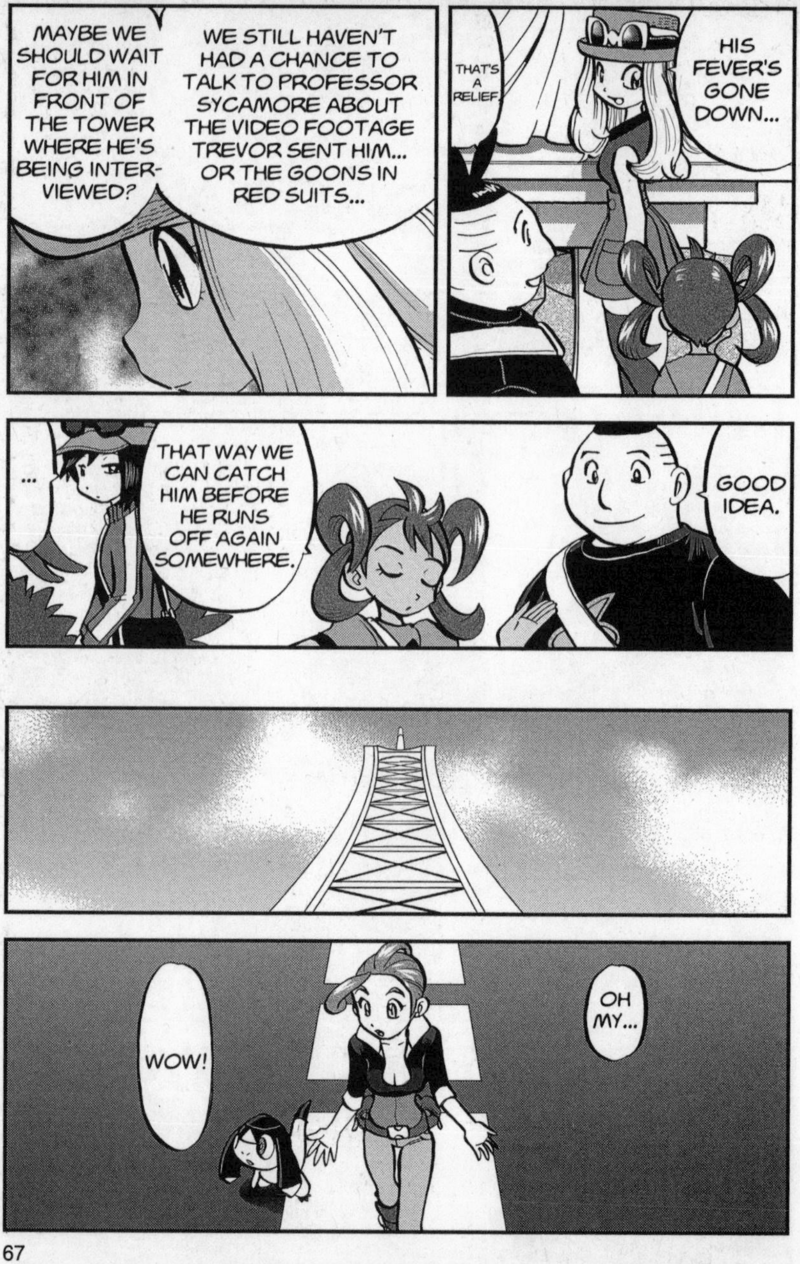
HIS FEVER'S GONE DOWN...
THAT'S A RELIEF.
WE STILL HAVEN'T HAD A CHANCE TO TALK TO PROFESSOR SYCAMORE ABOUT THE VIDEO FOOTAGE TREVOR SENT HIM... OR THE GOONS IN RED SUITS...
MAYBE WE SHOULD WAIT FOR HIM IN FRONT OF THE TOWER WHERE HE'S BEING INTER-VIEWED?
GOOD IDEA.
THAT WAY WE CAN CATCH HIM BEFORE HE RUNS OFF AGAIN SOMEWHERE.
...
OH MY...
WOW!

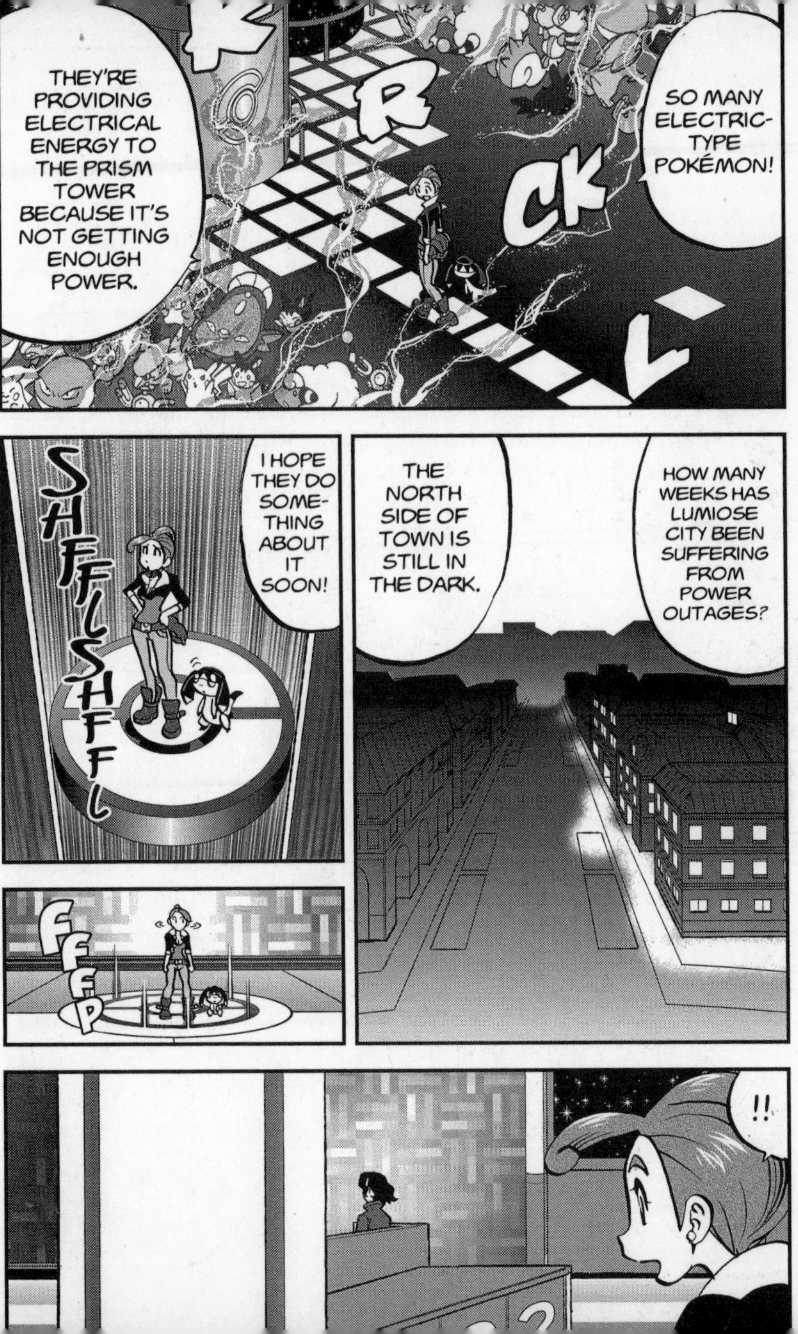
SO MANY ELECTRIC-TYPE POKÉMON!
R
CK
L
THEY'RE PROVIDING ELECTRICAL ENERGY TO THE PRISM TOWER BECAUSE IT'S NOT GETTING ENOUGH POWER.
HOW MANY WEEKS HAS LUMIOSE CITY BEEN SUFFERING FROM POWER OUTAGES?
THE NORTH SIDE OF TOWN IS STILL IN THE DARK.
I HOPE THEY DO SOMETHING ABOUT IT SOON!
SHFFL SHFFL
FFFP
!!

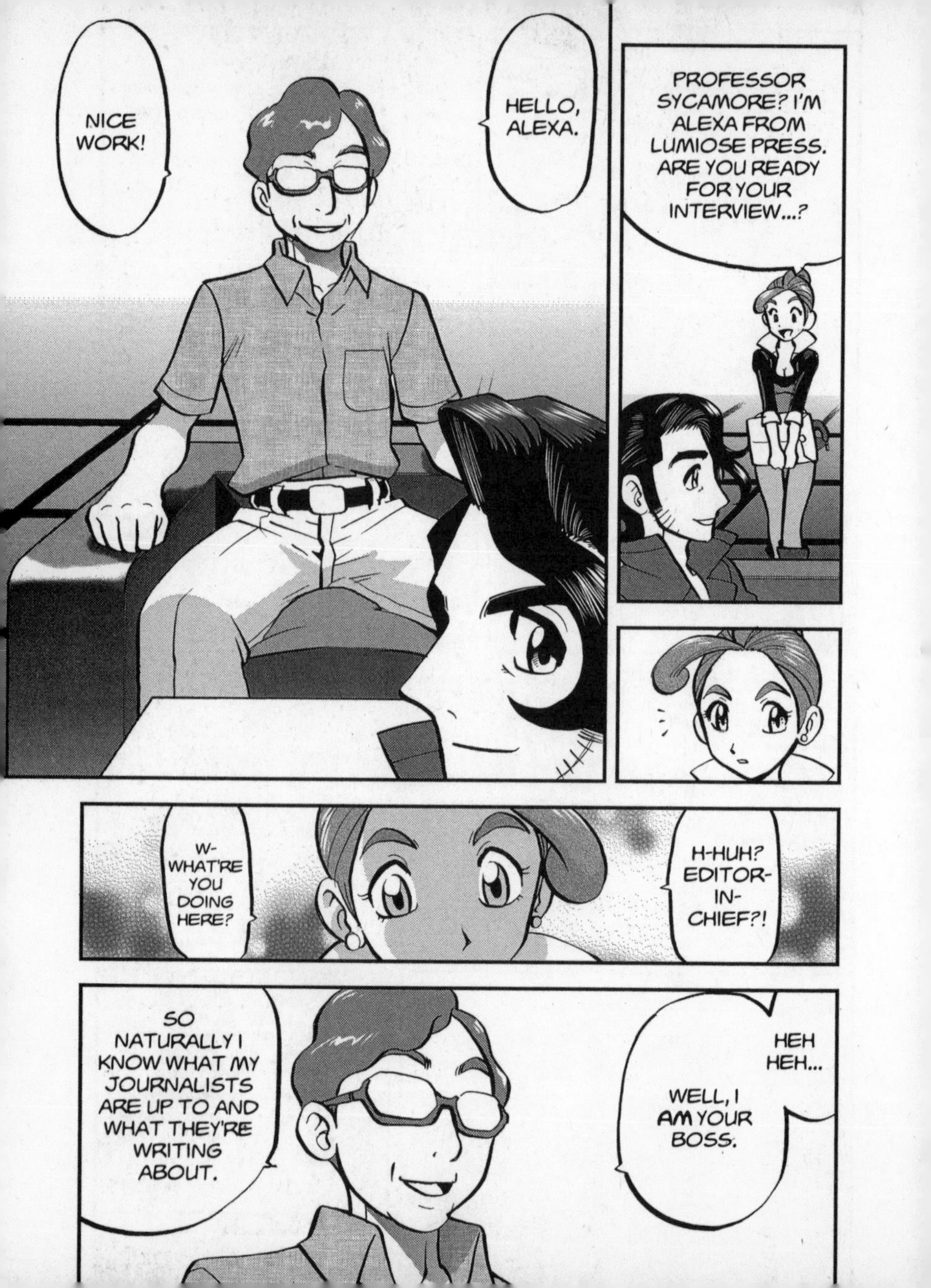
PROFESSOR SYCAMORE? I'M ALEXA FROM LUMIOSE PRESS. ARE YOU READY FOR YOUR INTERVIEW...?
HELLO, ALEXA.
NICE WORK!
H-HUH? EDITOR-IN-CHIEF?!
W-WHAT'RE YOU DOING HERE?
HEH HEH...
WELL, I AM YOUR BOSS.
SO NATURALLY I KNOW WHAT MY JOURNALISTS ARE UP TO AND WHAT THEY'RE WRITING ABOUT.

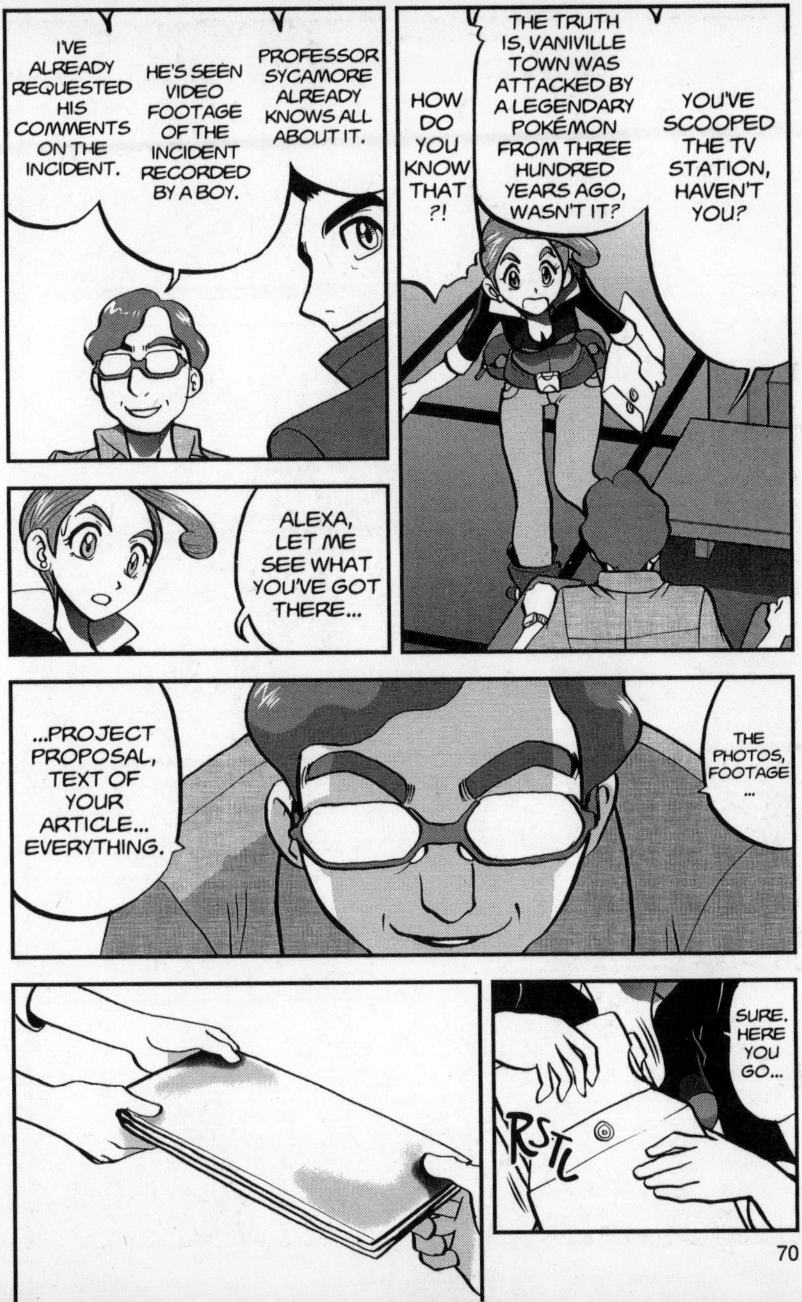
YOU'VE SCOOPED THE TV STATION, HAVEN'T YOU?
THE TRUTH IS, VANIVILLE TOWN WAS ATTACKED BY A LEGENDARY POKÉMON FROM THREE HUNDRED YEARS AGO, WASN'T IT?
HOW DO YOU KNOW THAT ?!
PROFESSOR SYCAMORE ALREADY KNOWS ALL ABOUT IT.
HE'S SEEN VIDEO FOOTAGE OF THE INCIDENT RECORDED BY A BOY.
I'VE ALREADY REQUESTED HIS COMMENTS ON THE INCIDENT.
ALEXA, LET ME SEE WHAT YOU'VE GOT THERE...
THE PHOTOS, FOOTAGE ...
...PROJECT PROPOSAL, TEXT OF YOUR ARTICLE... EVERYTHING.
SURE. HERE YOU GO...
RSTL

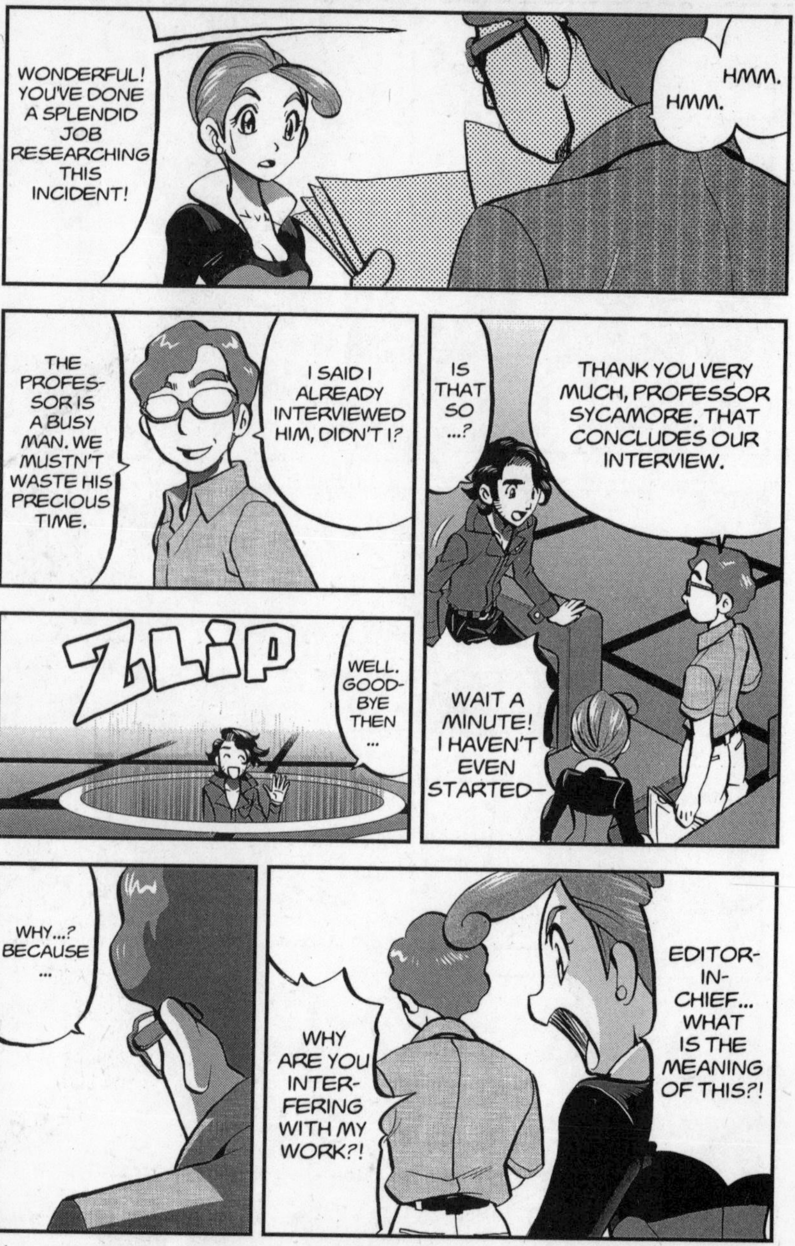
HMM. HMM.
WONDERFUL! YOU'VE DONE A SPLENDID JOB RESEARCHING THIS INCIDENT!
THANK YOU VERY MUCH, PROFESSOR SYCAMORE. THAT CONCLUDES OUR INTERVIEW.
IS THAT SO ...?
WAIT A MINUTE! I HAVEN'T EVEN STARTED—
I SAID I ALREADY INTERVIEWED HIM, DIDN'T I?
THE PROFES-SOR IS A BUSY MAN. WE MUSTN'T WASTE HIS PRECIOUS TIME.
WELL. GOOD-BYE THEN ...
ZLIP
EDITOR-IN-CHIEF... WHAT IS THE MEANING OF THIS?!
WHY ARE YOU INTER-FERING WITH MY WORK?!
WHY...? BECAUSE ...

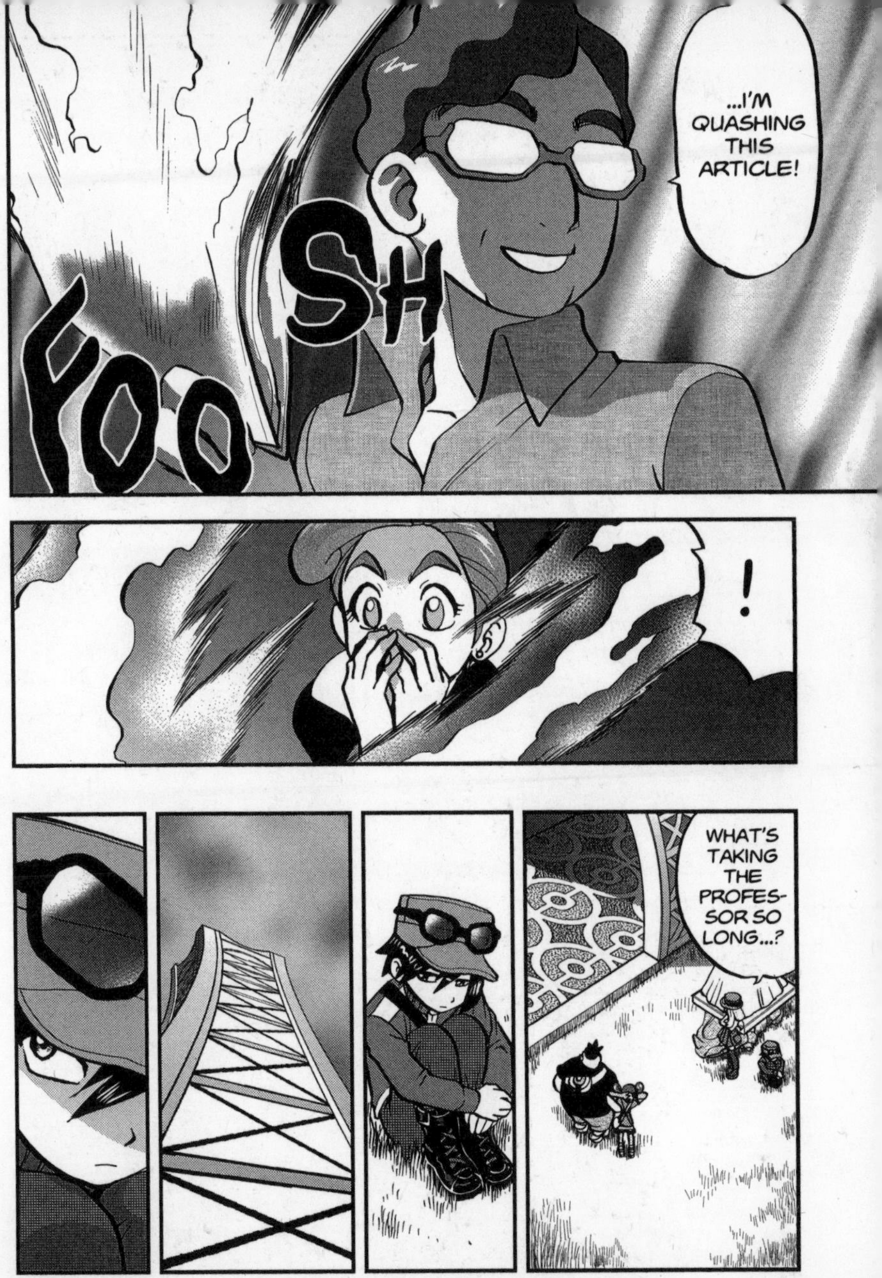
...I'M QUASHING THIS ARTICLE!
SH
FOOO
!
WHAT'S TAKING THE PROFES-SOR SO LONG...?

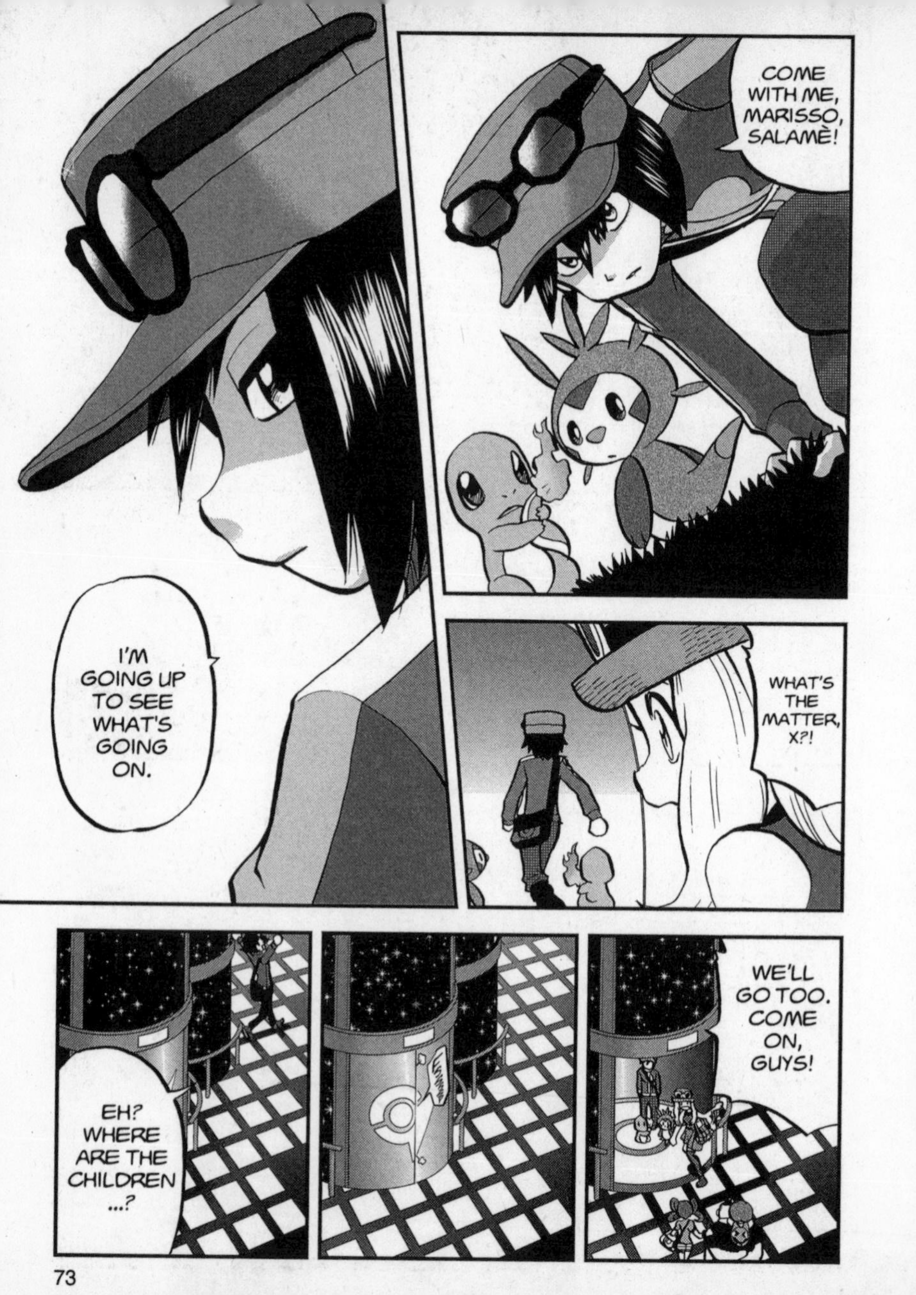

COME WITH ME, MARISSO, SALAMÈ!
WHAT'S THE MATTER, X?!
I'M GOING UP TO SEE WHAT'S GOING ON.
WE'LL GO TOO. COME ON, GUYS!
EH? WHERE ARE THE CHILDREN ...?

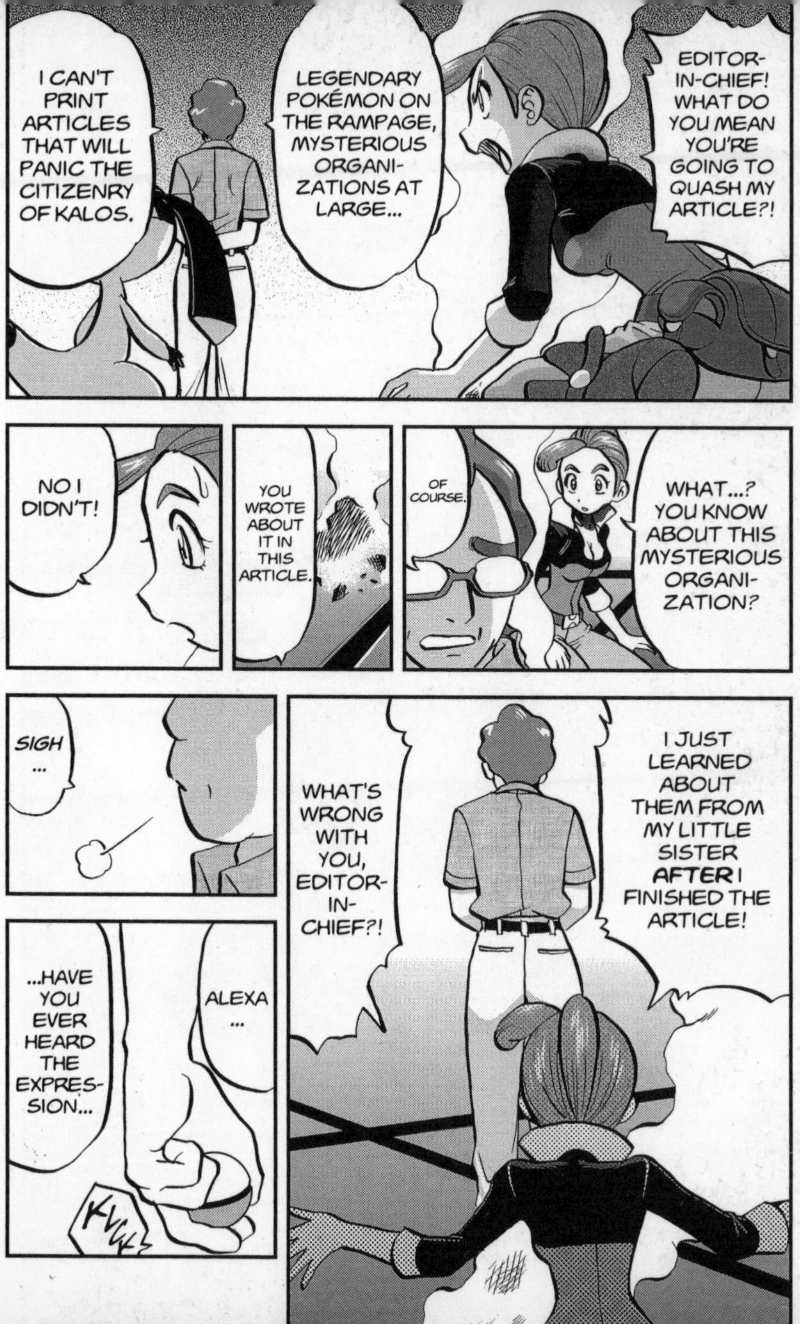
EDITOR-IN-CHIEF! WHAT DO YOU MEAN YOU'RE GOING TO QUASH MY ARTICLE?!
LEGENDARY POKÉMON ON THE RAMPAGE, MYSTERIOUS ORGANIZATIONS AT LARGE...
I CAN'T PRINT ARTICLES THAT WILL PANIC THE CITIZENRY OF KALOS.
WHAT...? YOU KNOW ABOUT THIS MYSTERIOUS ORGANIZATION?
OF COURSE.
YOU WROTE ABOUT IT IN THIS ARTICLE.
NO I DIDN'T!
I JUST LEARNED ABOUT THEM FROM MY LITTLE SISTER **AFTER** I FINISHED THE ARTICLE!
WHAT'S WRONG WITH YOU, EDITOR-IN-CHIEF?!
SIGH...
ALEXA...
...HAVE YOU EVER HEARD THE EXPRESSION...
KLICK

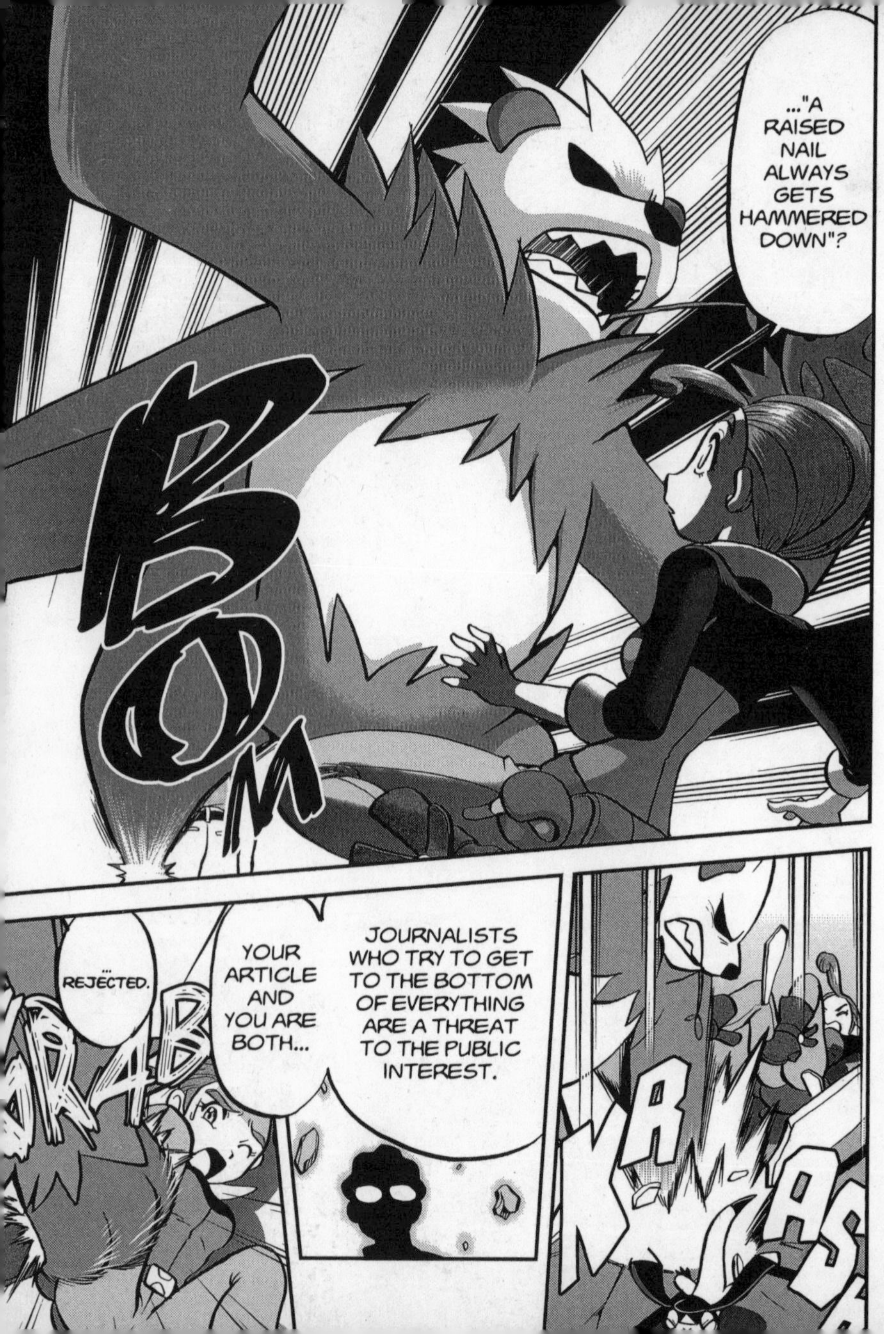
..."A RAISED NAIL ALWAYS GETS HAMMERED DOWN"?
BOOM
JOURNALISTS WHO TRY TO GET TO THE BOTTOM OF EVERYTHING ARE A THREAT TO THE PUBLIC INTEREST.
YOUR ARTICLE AND YOU ARE BOTH...
... REJECTED.

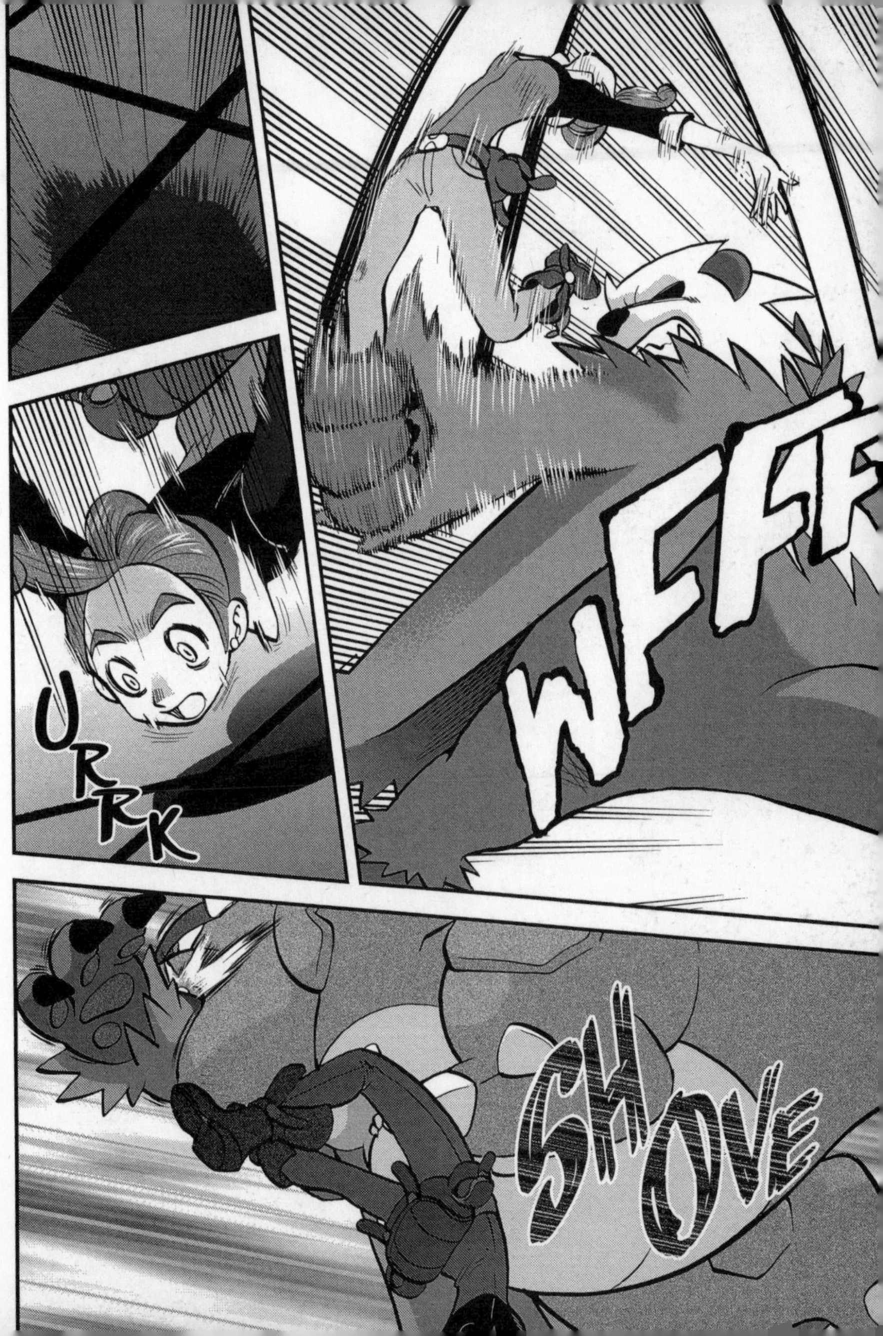
WFFF
URRK
SHOVE

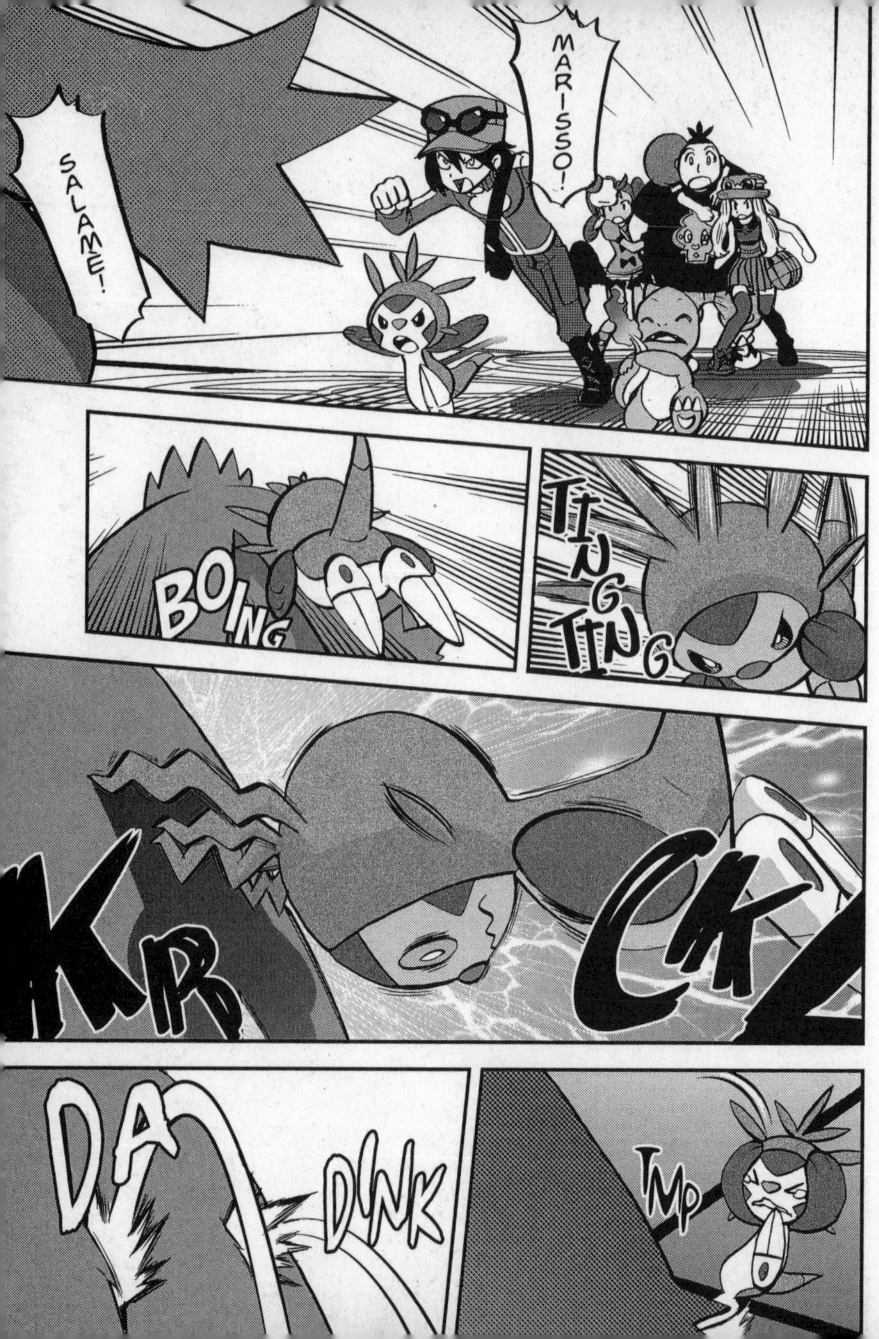

MARISSO!
SALAME!
TING
TING
BOING
KR
CK
TMP
DA
DINK

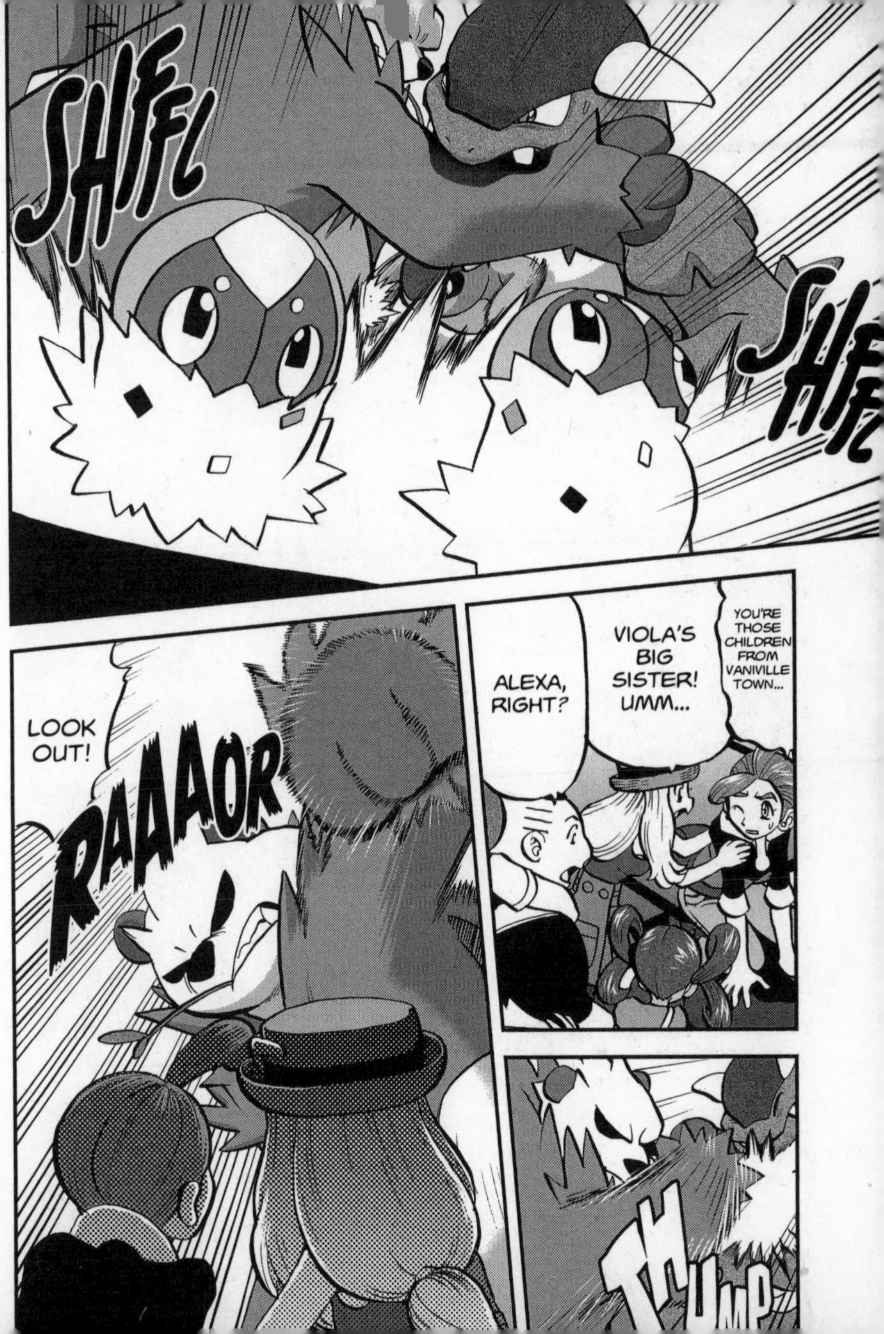
SHFFL
SHFFL
YOU'RE THOSE CHILDREN FROM VANIVILLE TOWN...
VIOLA'S BIG SISTER! UMM...
ALEXA, RIGHT?
THUMP
LOOK OUT!
RAAAOR

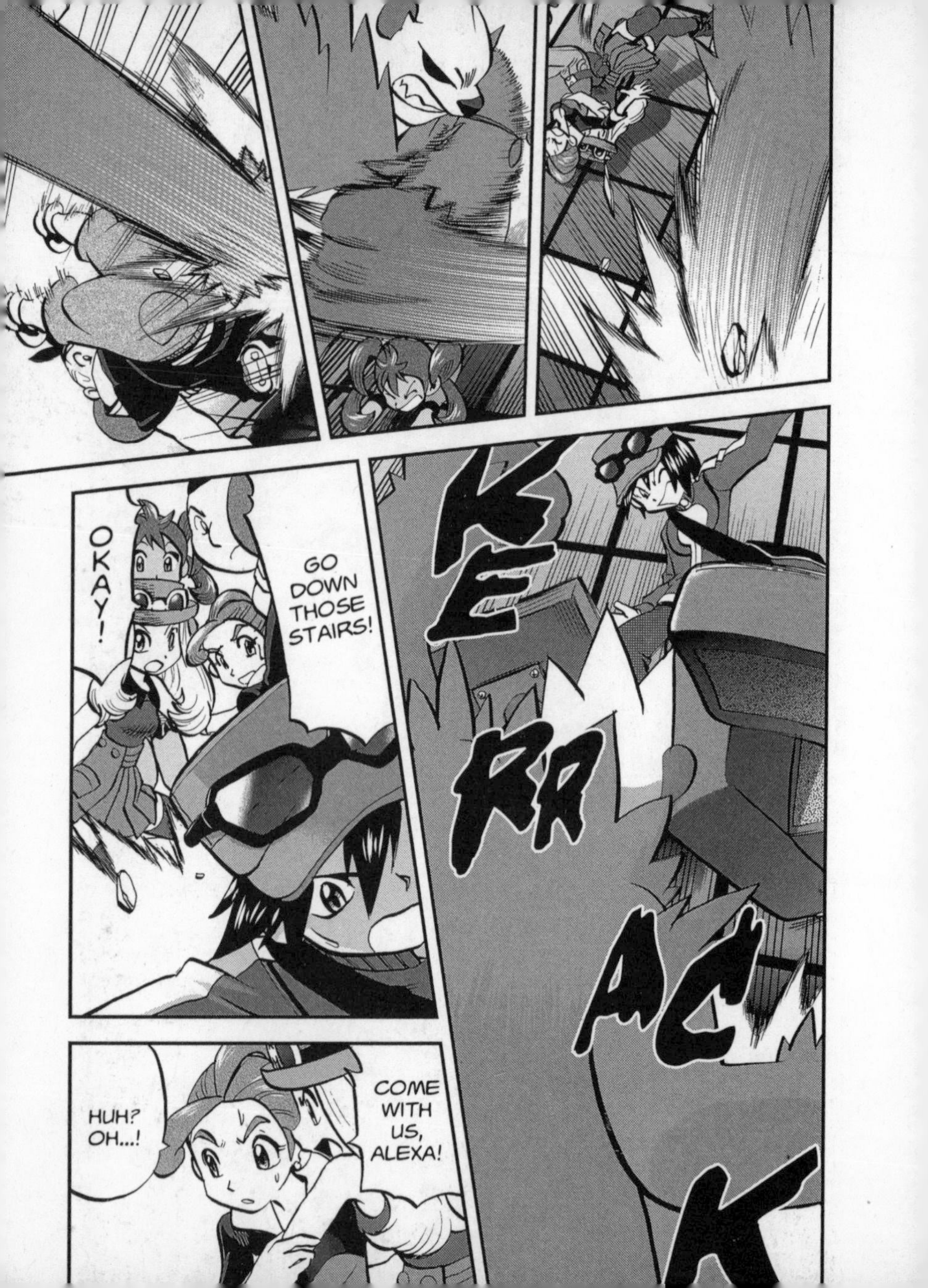
KERRACK
GO DOWN THOSE STAIRS!
OKAY!
COME WITH US, ALEXA!
HUH? OH...!

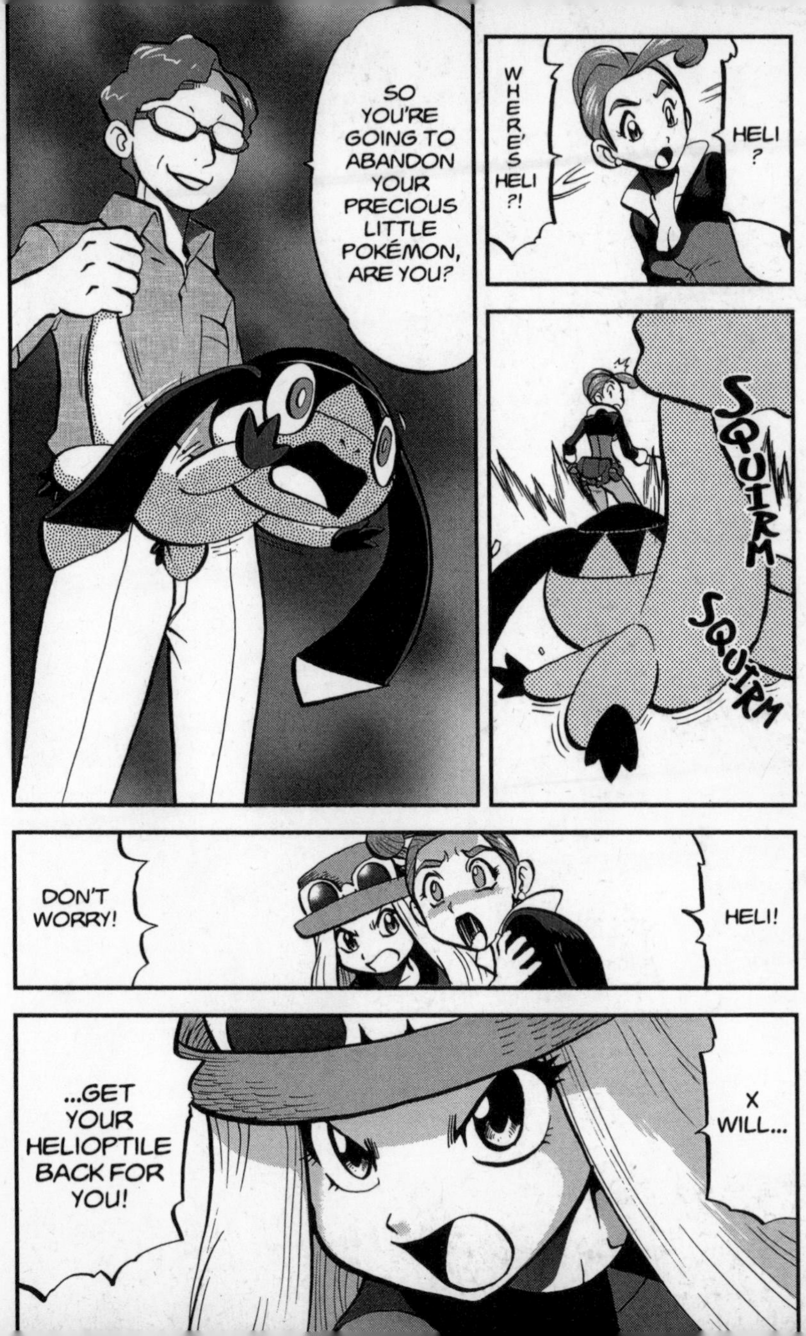
HELI ?
WHERE'S HELI ?!
SQUIRM SQUIRM SQUIRM
SO YOU'RE GOING TO ABANDON YOUR PRECIOUS LITTLE POKÉMON, ARE YOU?
HELI!
DON'T WORRY!
X WILL...
...GET YOUR HELIOPTILE BACK FOR YOU!

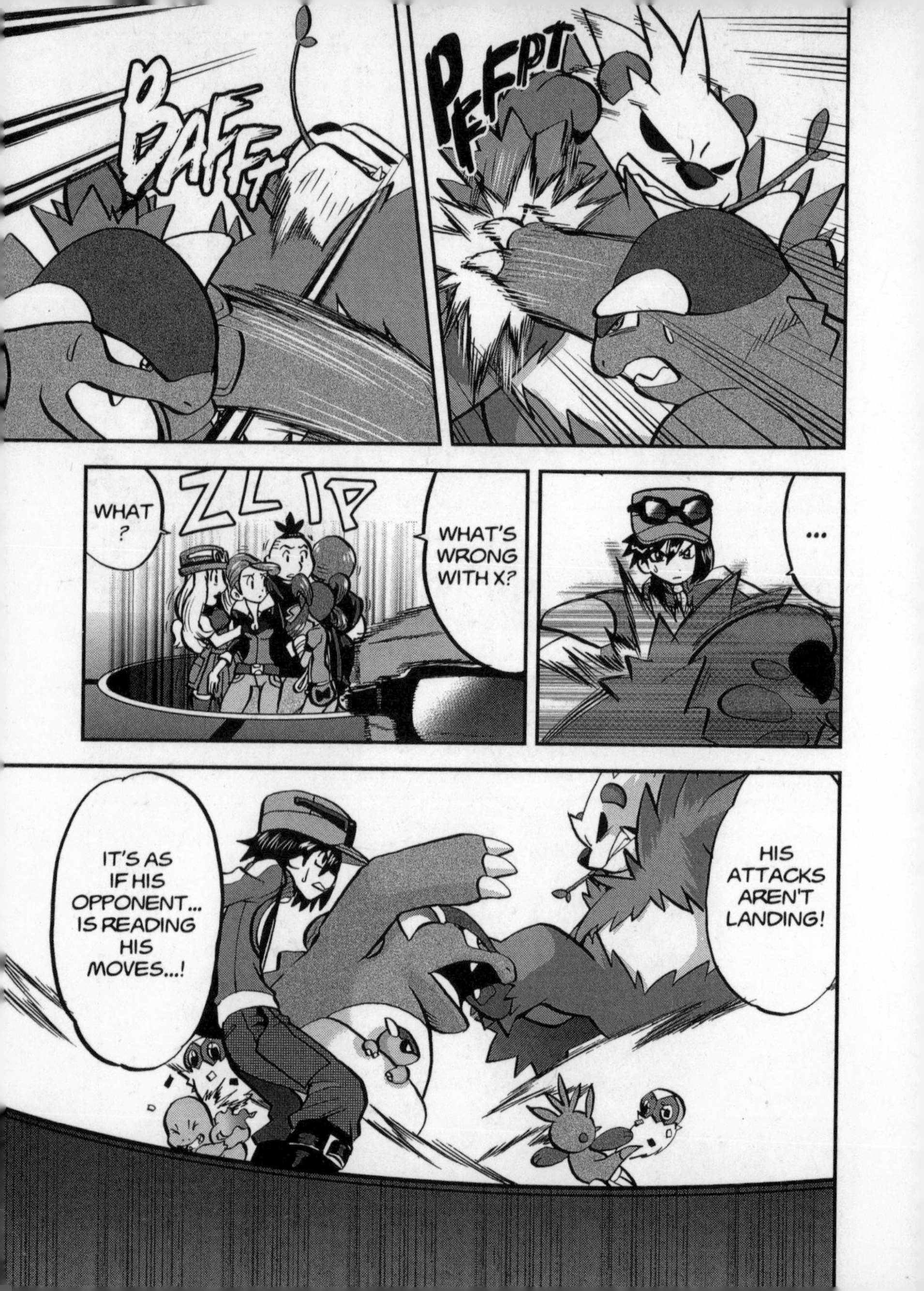
PFFPT
BAFFT
...
WHAT'S WRONG WITH X?
ZZIP
WHAT?
HIS ATTACKS AREN'T LANDING!
IT'S AS IF HIS OPPONENT... IS READING HIS MOVES...!

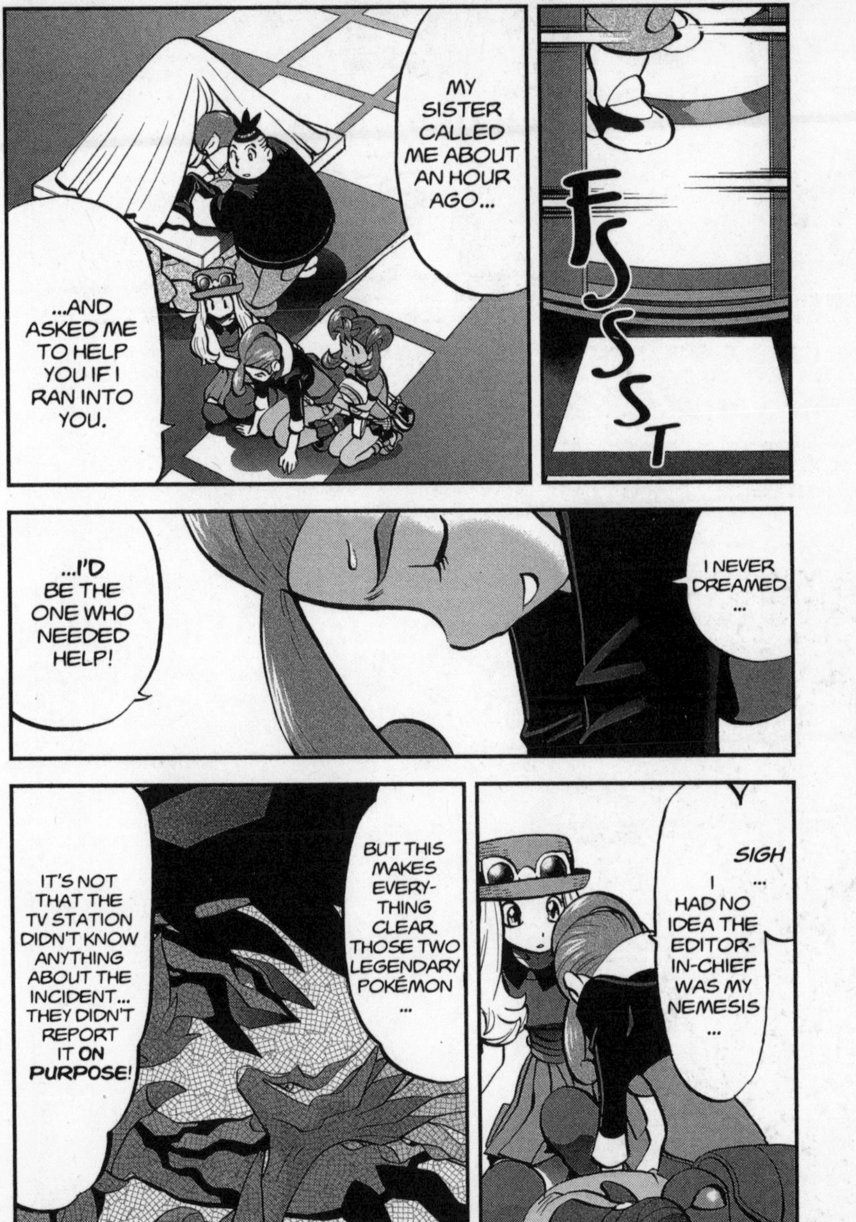
FSSST
MY SISTER CALLED ME ABOUT AN HOUR AGO...
...AND ASKED ME TO HELP YOU IF I RAN INTO YOU.
I NEVER DREAMED...
...I'D BE THE ONE WHO NEEDED HELP!
SIGH...
I HAD NO IDEA THE EDITOR-IN-CHIEF WAS MY NEMESIS...
BUT THIS MAKES EVERY-THING CLEAR. THOSE TWO LEGENDARY POKÉMON...
IT'S NOT THAT THE TV STATION DIDN'T KNOW ANYTHING ABOUT THE INCIDENT... THEY DIDN'T REPORT IT ON PURPOSE!

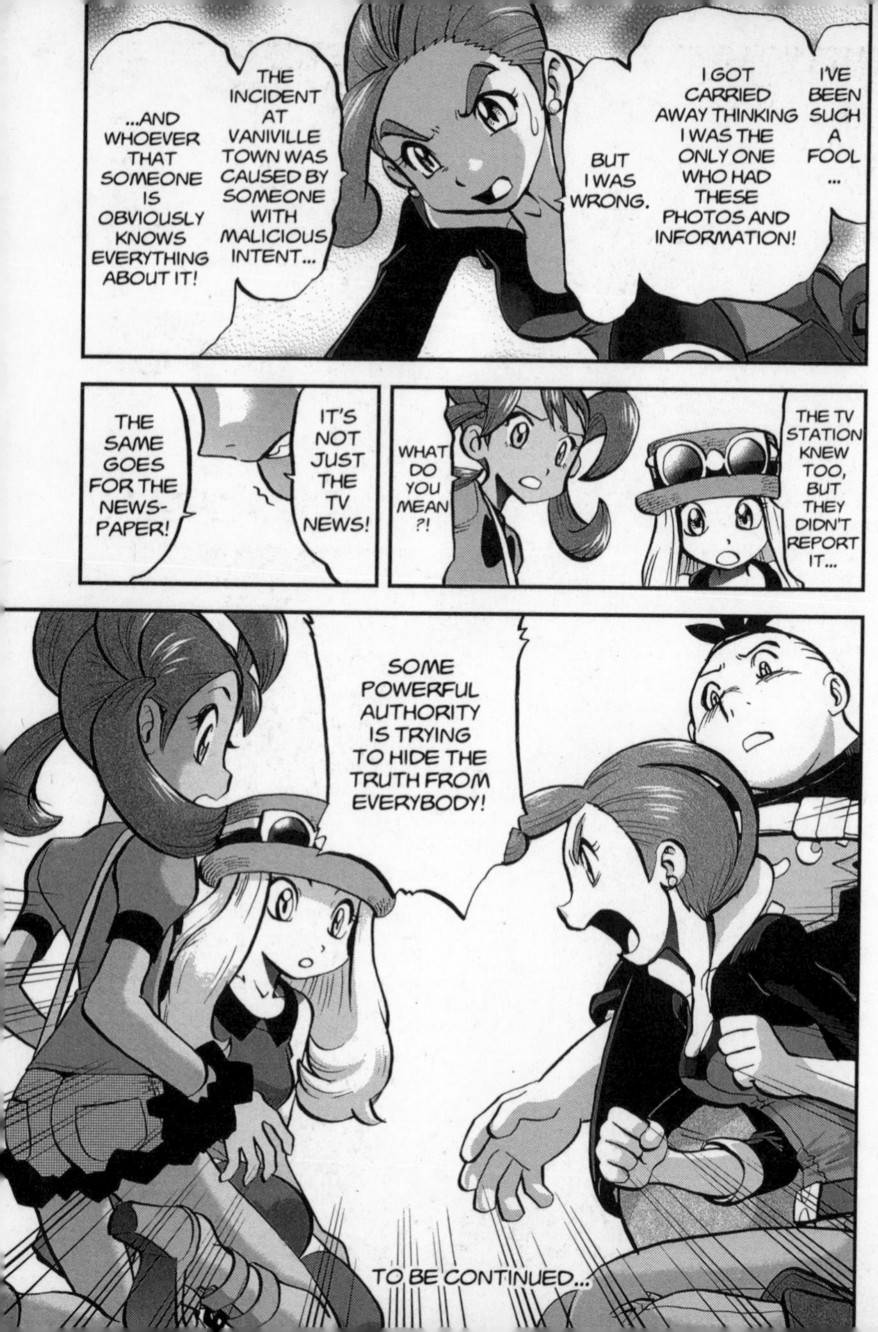
I'VE BEEN SUCH A FOOL...
I GOT CARRIED AWAY THINKING I WAS THE ONLY ONE WHO HAD THESE PHOTOS AND INFORMATION!
BUT I WAS WRONG.
THE INCIDENT AT VANIVILLE TOWN WAS CAUSED BY SOMEONE WITH MALICIOUS INTENT...
...AND WHOEVER THAT SOMEONE IS OBVIOUSLY KNOWS EVERYTHING ABOUT IT!
THE TV STATION KNEW TOO, BUT THEY DIDN'T REPORT IT...
WHAT DO YOU MEAN?!
IT'S NOT JUST THE TV NEWS!
THE SAME GOES FOR THE NEWSPAPER!
SOME POWERFUL AUTHORITY IS TRYING TO HIDE THE TRUTH FROM EVERYBODY!
TO BE CONTINUED...

## Current Location

**Lumiose City**

A dazzling metropolis of art and artifice, located in the very heart of the Kalos region.

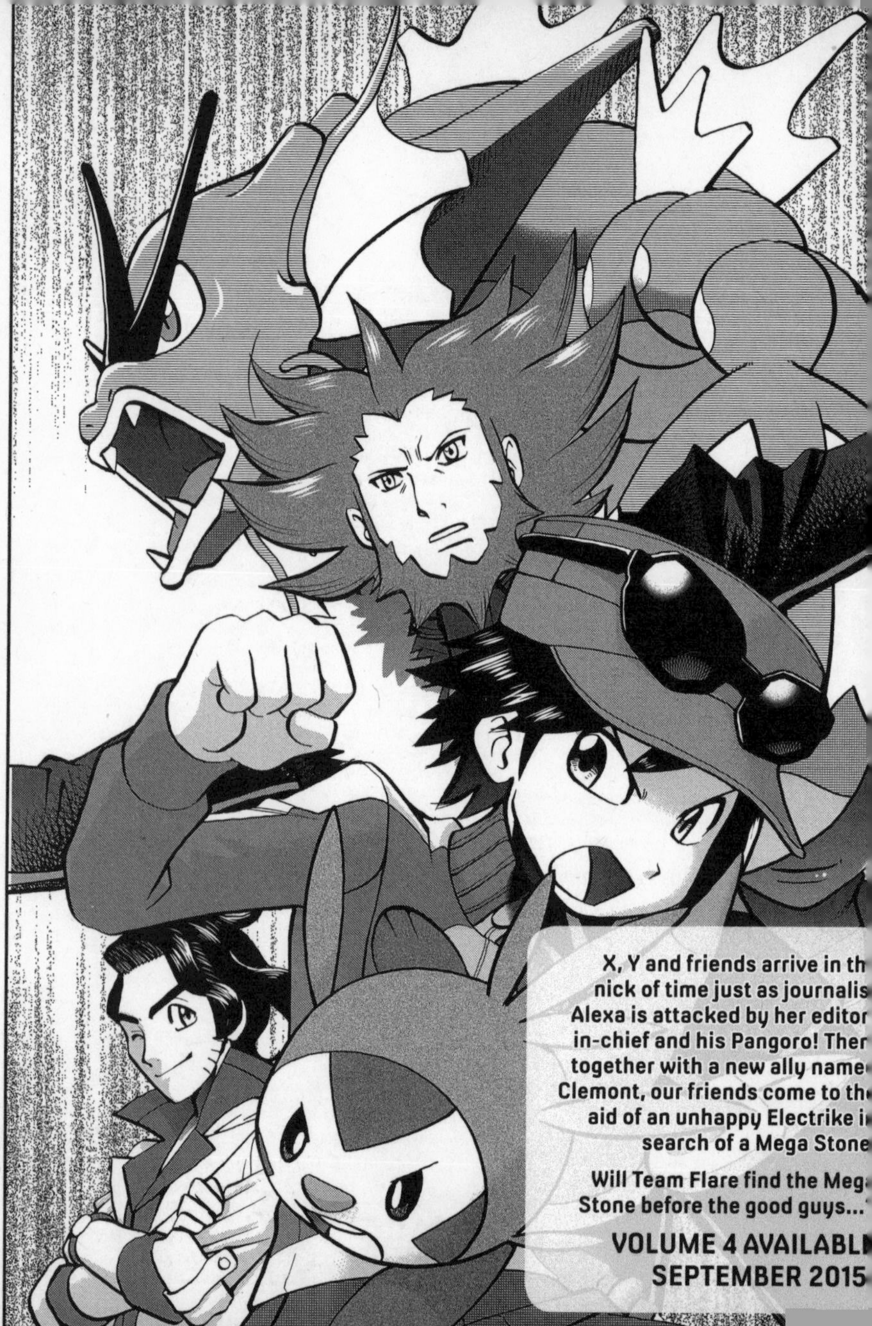
X, Y and friends arrive in th
nick of time just as journalis
Alexa is attacked by her editor
in-chief and his Pangoro! Ther
together with a new ally name
Clemont, our friends come to th
aid of an unhappy Electrike i
search of a Mega Stone
Will Team Flare find the Meg
Stone before the good guys...
VOLUME 4 AVAILABL
SEPTEMBER 2015

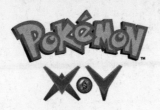

**Pokémon X • Y**
**Volume 3**
**Perfect Square Edition**

Story by HIDENORI KUSAKA
Art by SATOSHI YAMAMOTO

© 2015 Pokémon.
© 1995-2015 Nintendo/Creatures Inc./GAME FREAK inc.
TM, ®, and character names are trademarks of Nintendo.
POCKET MONSTERS SPECIAL X•Y Vol. 2
by Hidenori KUSAKA, Satoshi YAMAMOTO
© 2014 Hidenori KUSAKA, Satoshi YAMAMOTO
All rights reserved.
Original Japanese edition published by SHOGAKUKAN.
English translation rights in the United States of America, Canada, the United
Kingdom, Ireland, Australia and New Zealand arranged with SHOGAKUKAN.

**English Adaptation**—Bryant Turnage
**Translation**—Tetsuichiro Miyaki
**Touch-up & Lettering**—Annaliese Christman
**Design**—Shawn Carrico
**Editor**—Annette Roman

The stories, characters and incidents mentioned
in this publication are entirely fictional.

Printed in the U.S.A.

Published by
VIZ Media, LLC
P.O. Box 77010
San Francisco, CA 94107

10 9 8 7 6 5 4 3 2 1
First printing, June 2015

www.perfectsquare.com

www.viz.com

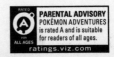
**PARENTAL ADVISORY**
POKÉMON ADVENTURES
is rated A and is suitable
for readers of all ages.
ratings.viz.com

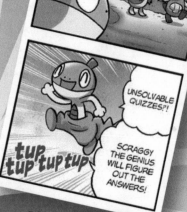
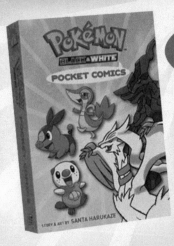

**Begin your Pokémon Adventure here in the Kanto region!**

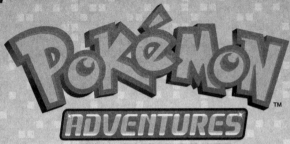

# POKÉMON™ ADVENTURES

## RED & BLUE BOX SET

Story by HIDENORI KUSAKA Art by MATO

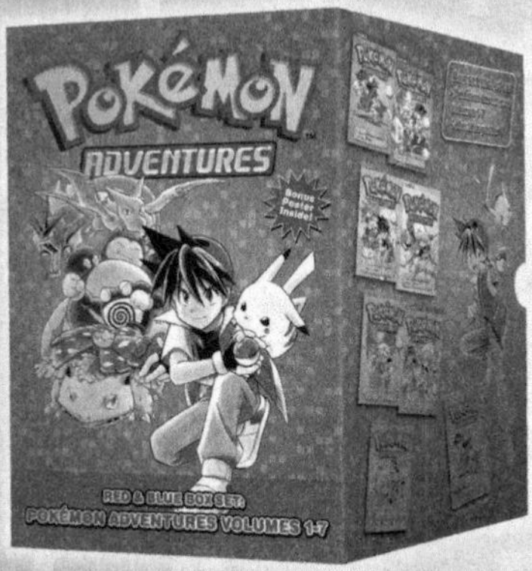
POKÉMON
ADVENTURES
Bonus Poster Inside!
RED & BLUE BOX SET:
POKÉMON ADVENTURES VOLUMES 1-7

Includes POKÉMON ADVENTURES Vols. 1-7 and a collectible poster!

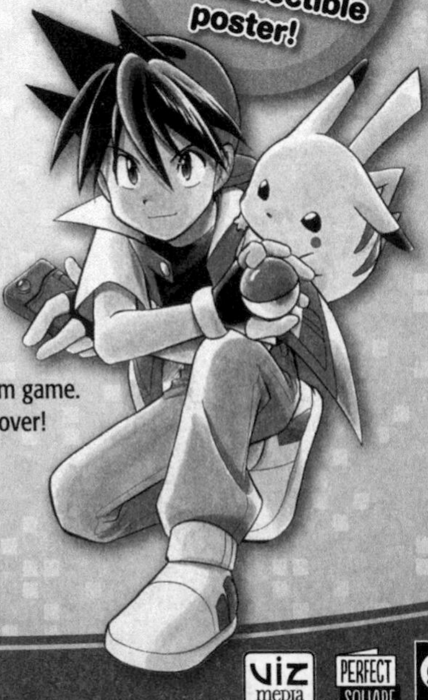

**All your favorite Pokémon game characters jump out of the screen into the pages of this action-packed manga!**

Red doesn't just want to train Pokémon, he wants to be their friend too. Bulbasaur and Poliwhirl seem game. But independent Pikachu won't be so easy to win over!

And watch out for Team Rocket, Red... They only want to be your enemy!

***Start the adventure today!***



VIZ media www.viz.com

PERFECT SQUARE

RATED A ALL AGES ratings.viz.com

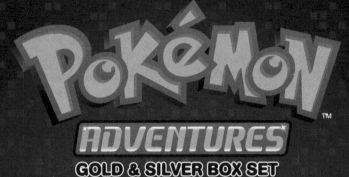

# POKÉMON ADVENTURES
## GOLD & SILVER BOX SET

Includes
**POKÉMON ADVENTURES**
Vols. 8-14
and a collectible poster!

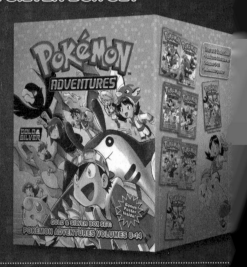

Story by
**HIDENORI KUSAKA**

Art by
**MATO,
SATOSHI YAMAMOTO**

More exciting Pokémon adventures starring Gold and his rival Silver! First someone steal Gold's backpack full of Poké Balls (and Pokémon!). Then someone steals Prof. Elm's Totod Can Gold catch the thief—or thieves?!

Keep an eye on Team Rocket, Gold... Could they be behind this crime wave?

**viz media**
www.viz.com

**PERFECT SQUARE**

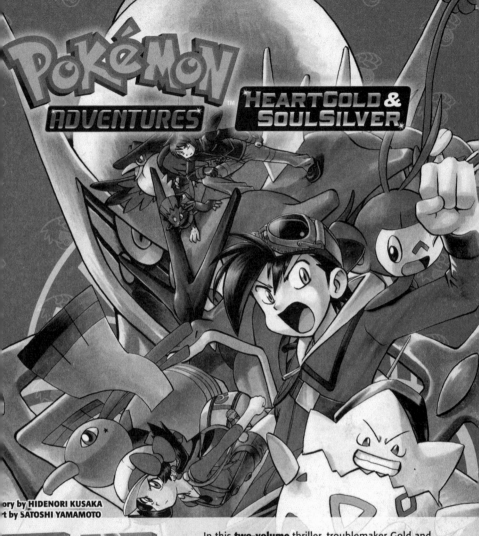

# POKéMON ADVENTURES™
## HEARTGOLD & SOULSILVER

ory by HIDENORI KUSAKA
rt by SATOSHI YAMAMOTO

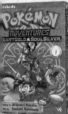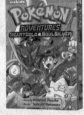

In this **two-volume** thriller, troublemaker Gold and feisty Silver must team up again to find their old enemy Lance and the Legendary Pokémon Arceus!

## Available now!

www.viz.com

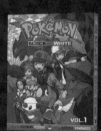

# Start the adventures in Kalos with Pokémon X·Y, Vol. 1!

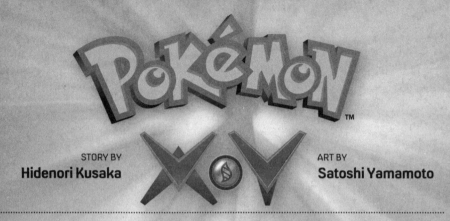

STORY BY
**Hidenori Kusaka**

ART BY
**Satoshi Yamamoto**

As the new champion of the Pokémon Battle Junior Tournament in the Kalos region, X is hailed as a child prodigy. But when the media attention proves to be too much for him, he holes up in his room to hide from everyone—including his best friends. Then, his hometown of Vaniville Town is attacked by the two Legendary Pokémon Xerneas and Yveltal and a mysterious organization named Team Flare!

*What will it take to get X to come out of hiding...?!*

## Only $4.99 US! ($5.99 in Canada)

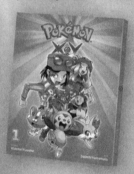

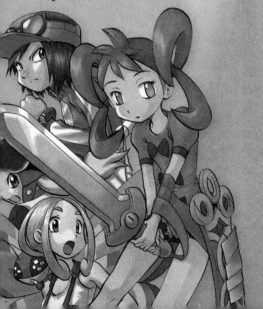

*Available at your local comic book shop or bookstore!*

**ISBN:** 978-1-4215-7980-1
**Diamond Order Code:** OCT141609

RATED
**A**
ALL AGES
ratings.viz.com

**PERFECT SQUARE**
www.PerfectSquare.com

**viz** MEDIA
www.viz.com

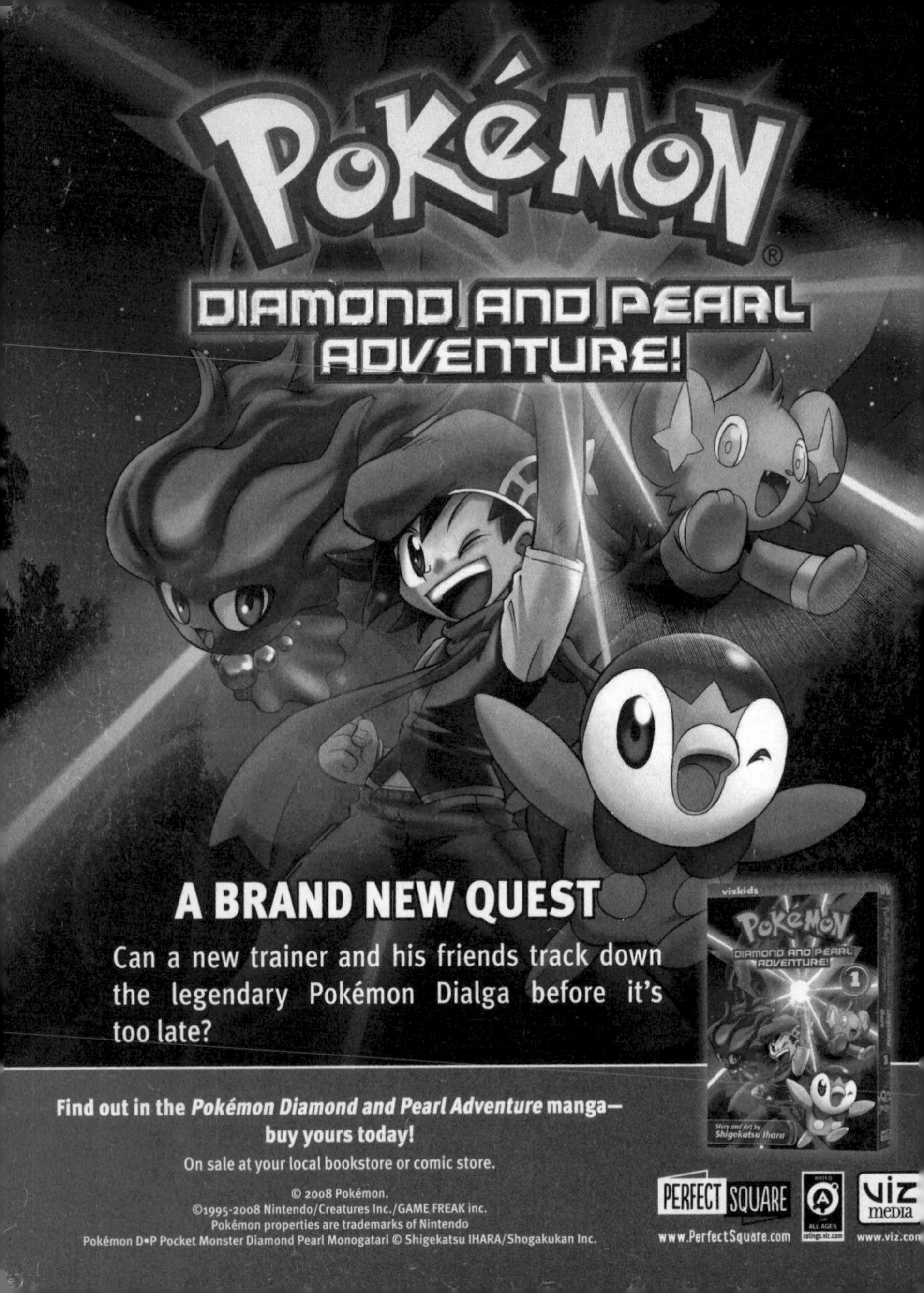
POKÉMON®
DIAMOND AND PEARL ADVENTURE!
A BRAND NEW QUEST
Can a new trainer and his friends track down the legendary Pokémon Dialga before it's too late?
vizkids
POKÉMON
DIAMOND AND PEARL ADVENTURE!
1
Story and Art by Shigekatsu Ihara
Find out in the Pokémon Diamond and Pearl Adventure manga—buy yours today!
On sale at your local bookstore or comic store.
© 2008 Pokémon.
©1995-2008 Nintendo/Creatures Inc./GAME FREAK inc.
Pokémon properties are trademarks of Nintendo
Pokémon D•P Pocket Monster Diamond Pearl Monogatari © Shigekatsu IHARA/Shogakukan Inc.
PERFECT SQUARE
www.PerfectSquare.com
ALL AGES
ratings.viz.com
VIZ media
www.viz.com

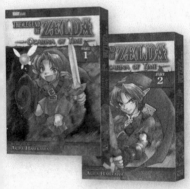
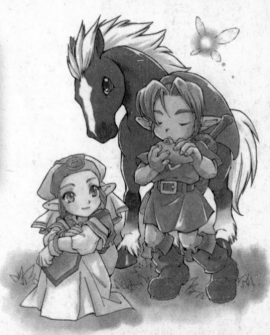

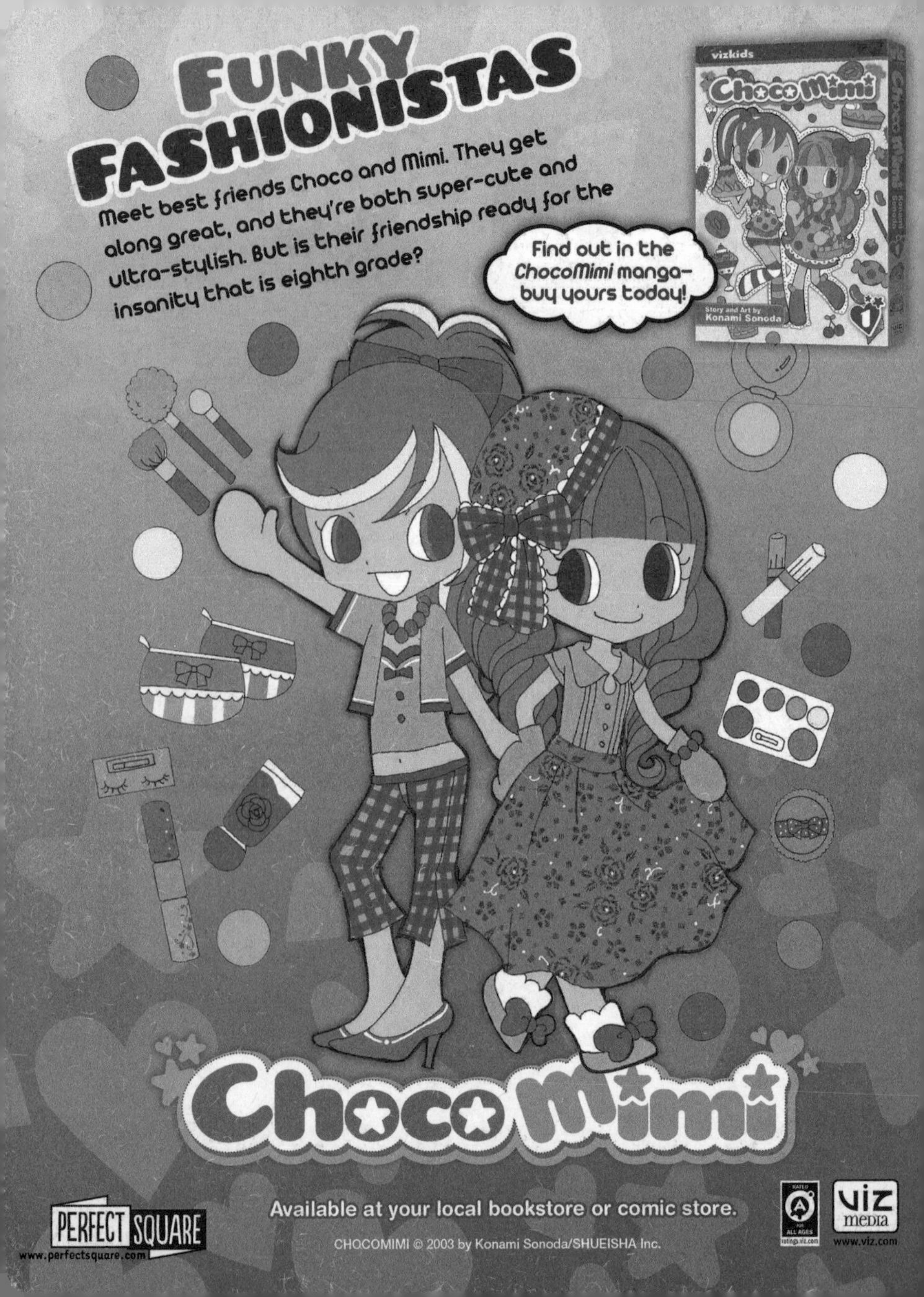
FUNKY FASHIONISTAS
Meet best friends Choco and Mimi. They get along great, and they're both super-cute and ultra-stylish. But is their friendship ready for the insanity that is eighth grade?
Find out in the ChocoMimi manga–buy yours today!
vizkids
Choco Mimi
Story and Art by Konami Sonoda
1
Choco Mimi
PERFECT SQUARE
www.perfectsquare.com
Available at your local bookstore or comic store.
CHOCOMIMI © 2003 by Konami Sonoda/SHUEISHA Inc.
VIZ MEDIA
www.viz.com

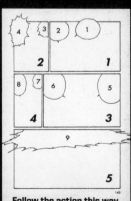

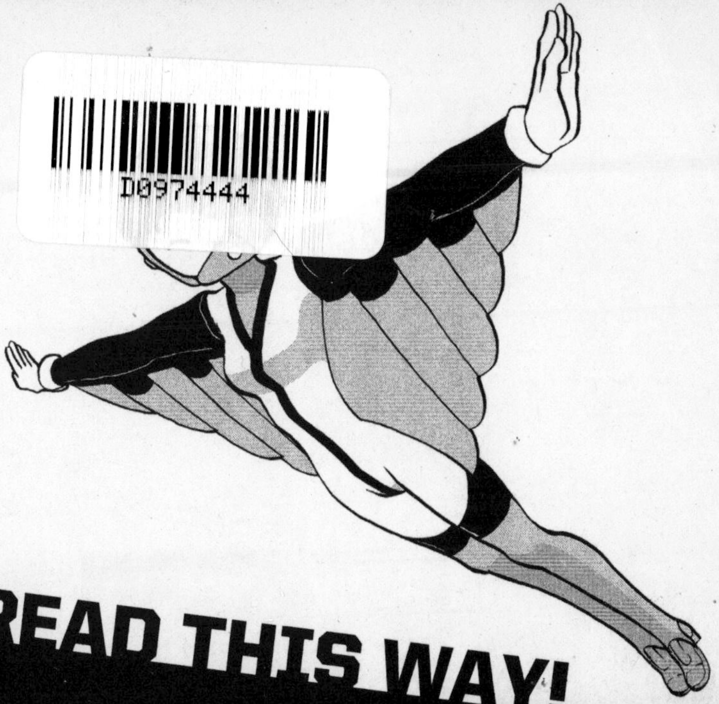

<<< **READ THIS WAY!**

## THIS IS THE END OF THIS GRAPHIC NOVEL!

To properly enjoy this VIZ Media graphic novel, please turn it around and begin reading from right to left.

This book has been printed in the original Japanese format in order to preserve the orientation of the original artwork. Have fun with it!

**Follow the action this way.**